With My Whole Heart

The Transformation

My heart is indicting a good matter; I speak of those things I've experienced with the King.

And I will never be the same.

By

Brenda A. Peacock

© 2003 by Brenda A. Peacock All rights reserved.

No part of this book may be reproduced, stored in a retrieval system, or transmitted by any means, electronic, mechanical, photocopying, recording, or otherwise, without written permission from the author.

ISBN: 1-4107-6884-8 (e-book)
ISBN: 1-4107-6883-X (Paperback)

This book is printed on acid free paper.

1st Books - rev. 10/27/03

Dedication

In loving memory of my mother Virginia, whom I miss dearly, but I thank God I know where you are. He made sure of that didn't He mom? I am who I am because of you. The things I've learned and the person I've become I owe to you. You taught me respect, to love my family and to care for others. You were with me for a season and when you had done all you could you departed giving place for still others to nurture me in areas (spiritually) where you couldn't. I have so much to learn in this Christian walk but you made certain the soil was fertile and ready for planting; for that I thank you mom. I will continue to grow into that woman God would have me be.

To my dad William, we call him Kilowatt (CB name), there is more to you than I realized. I'm so proud of you, and mom would be too. At times we can become so dependent on others that we don't reach our full potential. I've watched your love for Christ grow strong in these past years. Continue to share the gospel of Christ with everyone you meet. I thank you for being my dad and for always loving me.

To my sister Gwinda, we call her Gwin; you had to endure extremely difficult times in 2002, first the sudden home going of your beloved husband Marvin, and then our mom within a week. Through that I've watched as God transforms the caterpillar in you to a beautiful woman of God. There is strength in you that you've not yet tapped into, and it's that strength that I draw from. I admire your strength, courage and hope in Christ to continue on, and I thank God for you "baby sister."

Table of Contents

Dedication iii

Preface vii

My Love 1

A Treasured Journey 4

He Made Me 9

On The Cross 14

Show Me Your Glory! 19

The Peace Of God 26

My Warring Angel 34

I Lack Nothing 38

Abide With Me 43

His Face 48

An Ear to Hear 56

The Transformation 61

When I Need You Most 69

With My Whole Heart 87

When We Pray 93

PREFACE

Dear Readers,

My deepest desire is to encourage you to seek a closer and intimate relationship with the God who created us all.

> **This book was written in hopes that my Christian experience will inspire others to seek the face of Jehovah and to establish a sincere and personal relationship with our Lord and Savior Jesus Christ. There is so much of Him that he wants us to know. God is not satisfied with just a passive relationship or mediocre knowledge. He is seeking to become as one with us through His Son.**

Most Christian books are written to encourage others. Mine is no different but it is unique in that it reveals some of the wonderful things that only the Father and I have shared. I want to tell you of those experiences I've had with Abba, my Father.

Brenda Peacock

My Love

I have physically felt his love for me.
Not once, not twice, but three times honestly.
On his shoulders I found rest.
He laid his head beneath my breasts.
His mighty hand extended out.
The angelic host would carry it out.
Hanging on the cross I felt,
His life, he willingly gave himself.
My mind is fixed, and on him stays,
The woes of this world, I'll not lay prey.
All that I am or could be,
In his likeness, his image, he made me.
There is nothing in this world to fear,
If you have an ear, then hear.
I ride high as I journey.
I stand when facing the adversary.

Brenda A. Peacock

I proclaim the word of God,

Every day, anyway no matter what others say.

God has allowed me to feel His love, see his mighty hand and make known the un-searchable riches of His kingdom (righteousness, peace and joy in the Holy Spirit) through visions, dreams and revelation of His word.

This poem briefly reveals some of the dreams, visions, and experiences I've had with the Father. I will explain in more detail as we go, but first you must understand that God wants to make himself known to all. He is so……… that he can have a separate, unique, and intimate relationship with every believer, and I thank God that he is no respecter of persons.

We have a responsibility to share with others spiritual matters. God created us with a purpose and a plan. What a tragedy to spend our days in poverty and despair never receiving from Him that which he has ordained from the beginning. He longs to restore us to our rightful place in him.

His Love For Me
Let Him (God) kiss me with the kisses of His mouth: for thy love is better than wine. Draw me and I will run after thee: the King has brought me into His chambers: I will be glad and rejoice in thee, I will remember thy love more than wine. For many waters cannot quench love, neither can the floods drown it: if a man would give all the substance of his house for it, it wouldn't be enough, (Song of Solomon 1:1-2, 8:7).

Love is the very personality of who God is, His greatest attribute. No other word can adequately describe Him and that's not enough. The <u>BIBLE</u> reveals the true love and relationship God had/seeks with His chosen ones: love the Father has for his children (Exodus), a Husband for his wife (Hosea), and a Shepherd for his flock (Ephesians). It is that love we receive when we allow Jesus to live and reign in our hearts.

With My Whole Heart

God's plan for humanity was centered on that very principal, His love for mankind. That's who He is and all that He exhibits, for God is love (1 John 4:8), and there is nothing we can do to stop His love for us. You see, God loves the sinner but He hates sin. However when we refuse to receive Him as Lord in our lives we block the flow of grace that He so wants us to have.

God's love cannot be articulated, written on paper, etched on a canvas or envisioned in our minds, but is revealed in our hearts by the Holy Spirit, who teaches us all things. Our eyes have not seen nor can our ears hear but the Spirit testifies of the awesome love and existence of Almighty God. The Holy Spirit makes this deposit in our hearts if we (saints) allow Him. An understanding of His love for us allows us to walk in victory in this present world, but we continue to be defeated.

Satan, our adversary, knows something that the majority of the saints don't, and that is, he has absolutely no power over the believer. God asked me a very interesting question, "<u>Why do you fear Satan more than you trust me?</u>" The only answer I could give was, "I don't know." I would learn later that it's because we lack knowledge of His provisions for us. We are oppressed daily, fearing the attacks of the enemy more than trusting in the love God has for us. When we receive the revelation that "<u>Gods' love for us is more powerful than Satan's attack on us</u>" we will be that force that Satan cannot recon with. Jesus prayed in the Garden of Gethsemane (John 17:15) not that God should take us out of the world, but that He would protect us from the evil one (Satan).

It's time <u>the church,</u> which is the body of Christ, walk in and understand the love and authority given us. Then and only then will we walk in total victory over the enemy? Paul prayed that Christ may dwell in our hearts by faith (which works when we understand how much He loves us), we being rooted and grounded in His love, would comprehend with all saints what is the breadth, length, depth and height; and to know the love of Christ, which passes knowledge (Ephesians 3:11-19). For I have loved thee with an everlasting love: therefore with loving-kindness have I drawn thee (Jeremiah 31:3).

Brenda A. Peacock

A Treasured Journey

I have wasted many valuable years. I have searched high and looked low, walked near, and ran far. And where did it take me: over mountains and through valleys, across streams, and beyond the meadows. I wondered only to discover the answer to life is in Jesus Christ. I know not the curves in the road from afar but I travel with assurance that I have begun a journey in which there is no turning back. I can now count it all joy, this cycle of life that isn't always nice.

>Prayer:
>
>I thank you Father for the visions and dreams you've giving me.
>I thank you for a renewed mind that is stayed on you.
>I set my heart to obey you and to walk in your word.
>I acknowledge you, therefore, you teach me your ways.

This is My Story

During the early 90's I began to grow and mature in my walk with God. My job transferred me to Dallas, TX. There I joined a local church and became active in Bible study and Women auxiliary. Things were going good on the surface but inwardly I was headed for destruction. I was not happy nor had I been for many years. I was suffering from depression, and in times past suicidal thoughts.

I left my hometown several years prior, with the intention of severing ties with my family, that's how bound Satan had me. I was tormented with feelings of loneliness, self-pity, anxiety and all that is associated with the spirit of depression. I felt I didn't belong. What was my purpose and why am I here? I managed to suppress those thoughts for a while and continue with business as usual. I joined a local church and for the first time began growing in the knowledge of God. I watched Christian TV and was under good bible teaching, however I was suppressed by the cares of this world; those feelings of loneliness, self-pity and anxiety continued to rob me of the peace and joy that belonged to me as a believer. I didn't know how to cast my cares upon God, and wouldn't learn how until years latter.

Brenda A. Peacock

A Heart Message

I was told, and read, that God loves me.
But how could he, or anyone, you see.
Well, I was about to experience His love.
Not once, or twice, but three times honestly.
One night as I lay awake in bed,
Meditating on His word, he said.
I felt this pain across my chest,
That hurt so good I did confess.
The tears I shed as I clenched my chest
The joy of His love, it was the best.
I massaged my chest, and walked the floor,
I praised and danced more, more, more.

It was an incredible experience. As best I can explain, it was likened unto that of a throbbing massage, penetrating my very being. I laughed as the tears flowed down my cheeks. While clenching my chest, the Holy Spirit spoke, "This is how much I love you", and my response, "Lord You love me that much?" Don't you see how God loves me? But guest what? He loves you too.

No it was not a heart attack or any such thing. And for those inquiring minds, yes I've had three EKG's. Not as a result of my experiences but during regular checkups and yes, my heart is in excellent condition. And well shouldn't it be?

> ### *Psalm 17:3*
> A Prayer of David
> **Thou hast proved my heart; thou hast visited me in the night: thou has tried me and found nothing. I have purposed that my mouth shall not transgress.**

I've had that same experience on two other occasions while seeking God, and both times the presence of God filed my heart. God touched me and made known his love that left me at awes. I've felt his love for me and I'll never be the same.

God the Son left His throne in glory. The same (Jesus) was in the beginning with God (John 1:2). He stepped out of eternity and entered time. He laid aside His deity and put on humanity. Jesus became subject to creation, the very thing He Himself created. He made all things and without Him (Jesus) was not any thing made that was made (John 1:3). Then He who knew no sin became that thing (sin) that separated us from God. Yes!!!!! On the cross He bore it all, our transgressions, sins, iniquities, and imperfections so we don't have too. Ultimately, giving His life so that we might have life and reign eternally with Him. Why, because He loves <u>me</u>. Knowing and understanding His love is the key.

Each day as I draw nearer to Him, the more intimate we become, and the more He shares the mysteries of His kingdom (Mt. 13:11). "Many prophets and righteous men have desired to see and hear those things which you see and hear but have not seen them or

Brenda A. Peacock

heard them; but blessed are your eyes, for they see: and your ears, for they hear."

He Made Me

Hast thou not known? Hast thou heard? That the everlasting God, the Lord, the Creator of the ends of the earth faint not, neither is He weary? There is no searching of His understanding. He gives power to the faint; and to them that have no might He increase strength. Even the youth shall faint and be weary, and the young men shall utterly fall: but they that wait upon the Lord shall renew their strength; they shall mount up with wings as eagles; they shall run and not be weary; and they shall walk and not faint (Is. 40:28-31).

Father, I know you love me. Before you formed me in the belly, you knew me; and before I came out of the womb you sanctified me, and ordained me (Jer. 1:5). My very existence was predicated upon your divine plan to draw me unto yourself. You spared nothing in redeeming me, and I thank you. It has taken me years to respond to your calling but now I discern your sweet voice. In answering you, I have found my place in Jesus and through Him I'm set free. You brought me out of Egypt (bondage) and delivered me out of its hands, and out of the hand of all kingdoms (worlds systems), and of them that oppressed me (1 Sam 10:18). Oh, how gracious is your love toward me.

Father

To know you,
Is to love you.
And to love you,
Is to know Love itself.
You are Love.

What a time to be alive in Jesus. Time to awake to the calling for which we are called; have dominion and subdue planet earth (Gen. 2:26). The church is emerging from the dark shadows of despair and oppression and evolving as the victorious <u>body of Christ</u>. The Spirit of God is stirring the water like never before. And it shall come to pass in the last days, saith God, I will pour out of my Spirit upon all flesh: and your sons and daughters shall prophesy, and your young men shall see visions and your old men shall dream dreams (Acts 2:17). This: the acceptable time of the Lord.

I never imagined being where I am this day in Christ Jesus. I use to think I was born at least 50 years behind the times. I didn't feel I belonged. What was my purpose in life, why am I here? It has taken me years and deep soul searching to understand that God has purposed this, the end time for me/believers who will diligently search for Him. A people sold out to Him who will boldly declare, "The Spirit of the Lord is upon me for He has anointed me to share the <u>true gospel</u> to all." It is my time, and yes I was brought to the kingdom for such a time as this.

I was born and raised in a small southern town in eastern Arkansas, Forrest City, to be exact. I was the second of five children born to William and the late Virginia Peacock. I confessed a hope in Christ at an early age and attended church religiously. My church training was not uncommon to many of yours. I learned stories, quoted bible verses, heard songs of the life here after and sermons of fire and brimstone. I didn't understand that those teachings held a mystery that would later be unveiled, equipping me to walk victorious in this Christian journey.

Growing up in a Baptist church, my parents struggled, as did/does most saints. You couldn't tell us from the world. We were not taught that love freed us from the stronghold of the enemy: the bondage of lack, premature death, fear, oppression and such. I continued to be suppressed by the enemy until I began to seek God with all my heart and receive revelation of who I am in Him and the victorious life he purchased for me: the eyes of my understanding being enlightened; I know what is <u>the hope of His calling</u>, and what the riches of the glory of His inheritance in the saints (Eph. 1:18); that we being rooted and grounded in love, may be able to <u>comprehend what is the breadth, length, depth, and height of His love for us</u>.

Salvation Package

My first experience with the Holy Spirit was the day I accepted Jesus as my Lord and Savior. Upon that initial act of obedience I became one with Him, a joint heir with Christ. No more alienated from God but a son. I immediately received eternal life and the entire <u>salvation</u> package: freedom from the bondage in which Satan had (past tense) us.

Sunday June 23, 2000 my eyes (spirit) were enlightened as I began to receive understanding of that total salvation package. The Holy Spirit was dealing heavily with me to, "Press in and seek God because He is about to do something awesome in your life." That would turn out to be an understatement, eight months later. This was the beginning of the 1st day of my fast and I had never felt God's presence that strong before. Salvation was heavy on my heart. "I just want to hear from you God," I confessed, "Lord none of me but all of you." I immediately opened my bible to Is. 12:13, "Therefore with joy shall ye draw water (anointing) out of the wells of salvation."

Jesus spoke to the lady at the well, "Whosoever drinks this water shall thirst again: but whosoever drinks that which I shall give him shall never thirst again; but the water (anointing) that I shall give him shall be in him a well of water springing up into everlasting life (John 4:14)." The Holy Sprit living within us is that well (reservoir) whereby we draw water (anointing) to combat the evil of this world; healing from sickness and disease, breaking the bondage of poverty and lack, and restoring our position with the Father as co-ruler of the universe.

We are birthed into a new kingdom (system of operation) when we accept Jesus in our lives. Old things pass away (sick bodies, poverty, demonic strongholds and etc.) behold all things become new (divine health, prosperity, prosperous soul and etc.). The old nature, which was subject to the curse, dies and the new spirit man (liberated by Jesus on the cross) comes into being. We regain our rightful place with the Father: the <u>righteousness</u> of God in Christ Jesus and a joint heir with Him, thereby rendering Satan and all of his demonic forces subject to our authority (under our feet) by Christ Jesus.

> **He brought me in,**
>
> **To fill me up,**
>
> **Then send me out.**

God sent His Son, made of a woman, to redeem us from deaths' hold. Jesus won the battle against Satan and took back the keys to death and the grave so we wouldn't be subject, but rein victoriously with Him in heaven and on earth. "My children, I've given you the keys (access) to my kingdom (love, peace and joy in the Holy Ghost) and the gates of hell shall not prevail against you nor shall any weapon formed against you prosper. The keys are yours to use according to the wisdom, knowledge and understanding you acquire of me."

Jesus came as recorded by the prophet Isaiah (61:1-3) to reclaim that which was stolen, and to set us free: to preach good tidings unto the meek; to heal the broken hearted, preach deliverance to the captives, and recovery of sight to the blind, and the opening of

With My Whole Heart

the prison to them that are bound, to proclaim the day of vengeance of our God and to comfort all that mourn. Those provisions belong to us and will manifest in our lives when we know and understand the love He has for us, and have faith in His word (which works by our love for Him). Because you have set your love upon me and know my name, I will deliver you and set you on high. I will be with you in trouble and honor you. With long life will I satisfy you and show you my salvation (Ps. 91:14-16).

You see, God did not save me in order to lose me to a spirit of depression/suicide, which is how the devil came at me, or any other demonic force. He had a plan for my salvation (escape) that was methodically and strategically executed. A plan that was infallible. All bases were covered, every I dotted, every T crossed, and not one stone left unturned. No wonder He's Savior.

Sadly the church, which is the body of Christ, continues to allow the enemy to hold us captive, particularly in our minds. Few of us really know what we have in Jesus. Most Christians think it's okay to be broke, sick, and burdened with this worlds' system, which is of the devil. For what so ever is born of God over cometh the world: and this is the victory that over cometh the world, even our faith (1 John 5:4,5). Who is he that over cometh the world, but he that believeth that Jesus is the Son of God?

God has equipped us for battle and is watching our reactions to the trials of this life. Because I know I'll be victorious, I'm learning not to ask why the test but what is the lesson to be learned as a result of the test? In the midst of all the fiery darts, the greatest lesson I've learned is knowledge of His love for me, and it's because of that love I devote my whole heart to Him.

Brenda A. Peacock

On The Cross

"Oh how I love Jesus because He first loved me." If there was ever a truth that song tells of it. We were created in His love and because of His love. This world will never know that love because it is rejected daily. For what so ever is born of God over cometh the world: and this is the victory that over cometh the world, even our faith (1 John 5:4,5). Who is he that over cometh the world, but he that believeth that Jesus is the Son of God?

God loves us so, that He didn't leave it there. He made a way for us to come unto Him by way of the cross: the covering of the blood of Jesus. We were bought with a price but many have not accepted this free gift. And even more are those who have received the gift of redemption but have yet to open the package. Oh, you need to look in side and redeem those treasures that are forever more.

I accepted Christ at an early age, but my maturation has taken many years, and have by no means attained. If I had known then, what I now know, what a difference my life would be. I thank God for the good times and the bad, and I rejoice in the trials and tribulations He has brought me through. It was during those times that I learned who He was, what I have in Him, and what He means to me. Allow me to share my experiences with you.

"I didn't die for nothing"

God has allowed me to experience things that left me at awes, one of which was his love and endurance on the cross. I felt his tired shoulders as he bore the sins of the world, and the submission as he hung his head not in shame but in surrender (Phil 3:10). I was in church this particular night, myself and several other saints, praying and interceding for our pastor and members. We began with corporate prayer, touching and agreeing that the Father's will be done. As we separated, we began lying on of hands, and claiming territory that Satan was so desperately trying to steal. I found myself, or was lead to the baptismal pool where I began praying in the Spirit (with other tongues).

I felt my body literally being pinned to the wall; arms stretched shoulder width, hands opened out, and chin resting in my chest.

As I stood there, not realizing the position I was in, something incredible happened, the Lord spoke to me, "<u>I didn't die for nothing.</u>" When I became aware of what I was experiencing, I immediately cried out in travail.

Do we really know/understand what happened on the cross? No, we won't ever fully understand Jesus' ordeal on the cross, but what a perfect sacrifice. Our Easter rendition paints a passive picture of that life-altering event: Jesus being whipped, crowned with thorns, pierced in the side and finally declaring, "It is finished." These things did take place but it wasn't pretty or pleasant, it was a horrific scene.

Isaiah 53 gives us a more vivid picture of the crucifixion. The cross was the altar and the Son of God was the sacrificial offering. He was separated from the Father and became everything the

Father despised; sin. How many of you know sin is ugly? Knowing that, it stands to reason that Jesus appearance changed. His flesh was marred beyond recognition. Every disfiguration, disease, plague and evil attack known to man fell upon Him. Yes, every thing Satan could/would bring against mankind Jesus bore it on the cross so we don't have too.

Why Jesus? Why did you do it? Because you looked through the window of time and saw me returning to you, my first love, with all of my heart, soul, mind, and strength, "Crossing over unto the other side" (Mk 4:35), just as you instructed me during one of our times together. Being crucified with Christ: nevertheless I live; yet not I, but Christ living in me: and the life which I now live I live by the faith of the Son of God, who loved me, and gave Himself for me (Gal 2:20). Jesus gave His life that we might live with and through Him.

Back to the pool area, as I stood there for what seemed a very long time, my arms would not come down. I could barely feel them tiring. I experienced it a second time that night after reentering the sanctuary. I was sitting in the choir stand praying and my arms began to stretch out again as my head dropped.

The third time is always a charm, right? Yes, I had the "cross experience" a third time, three or four years later. God led me to join another church. During Sunday morning praise and worship, my dear friend Beverly, a true woman of God, received a prophetic word, "The Lord said when we began to truly praise Him He stands at attention." I saw, as she was speaking, the image of the Son of God standing tall and erect, dressed in a long white robe. Instantly I was filled with the spirit. My arms went out as my head dropped, resting my chin in my chest. Again, I wasn't aware of what was happening.

Lord, you counted the cost
For the souls that were lost
You paid the price
Your blood does suffice.

That I may know Him, and the power of His resurrection, and the fellowship of His sufferings, being made conformable unto His death; If by any means I might attain unto the resurrection of the dead (Philippians 3:10-11).

The Devils' Restraint

How does a fourth time sound? No, not really but I did experience something similar several years prior, but it was of the Devil. At the close of Sunday school the instructor asked for a volunteer to give the closing prayer. I all but hyperventilated at the thought of praying aloud. I could barely keep my composure as my breath shortened, my arms went down to my side, and I stood there with both hands and shoulders literally pinned to the wall.

I wasn't afraid but terrified of praying aloud. Satan knew it and fought to keep my prayer life dormant. Christianity is a relationship with God and our prayer life is the line of communication. It is our means of speaking to and hearing from the Father; therefore man aught to always pray. My prayer life left a lot to be desired, almost nonexistent, and Satan was trying his best to keep it that way. He will do all he can to block if not stop our communication with the Father. He knows that our Father in heaven hears and answers prayers. "I am a prayer warrior."

Man was made in the image of God, after His likeness (Gen 1:26). Given authority to reign over the earth, have dominion over all the works of His hands, and to talk with Him in the calm of the day. It grieves God to not have the kind of relationship with us that He purposed before we were created in the world. The relationship He shared with Adam and Eve in the Garden of Eden. "Then shall you call upon me, and ye shall go and pray unto me, and I will hearken unto you. And ye shall seek me, and find me, when ye shall search for me with all your heart. And I will be found of you, says the Lord: and I will turn away your captivity (Jer. 29:11-14)."

Brenda A. Peacock

Our life should be an example to this dying world that Jesus is the answer. God wants to reveal himself in phenomenal ways during these last days. He has not chosen a select few on the contrary He wants to touch every soul. Every believer who seeks to learn of Him, He promises to make Himself known. Thus says the Lord, ask me of things to come concerning my sons, and concerning the work of my hands. I have not spoken in secret, in a dark place of the earth. I have raised him up in righteousness, and I will direct all his ways (Is. 45:11,13a, 19a).

Show Me Your Glory!

I began writing this book over three years ago after receiving many visions and revelations from the Holy Spirit. I felt I had to share them. I had reached a point in my walk with God that I longed to know Him and to be close to Him. I began studying the word more intently and longed for a more intimate relationship with my Master. I had a hunger and thirst for Him, "God teach me your ways." "Let me see your face, show me your glory."

The glory of God is the very essence of his character, "<u>I AM THAT I AM</u>." In the book of Exodus 34:6-7, God revealed a small portion of Himself to Moses. He proclaimed, The Lord, The Lord God, merciful and gracious, longsuffering, and abundant in goodness and truth, keeping mercy for thousands, forgiving iniquity and transgressions and sin, and that will by no means clear the guilty: visiting the iniquity of the fathers upon the children, and upon the children's children, unto the third and to the fourth generation. This was not, by any means, all of who God was but all that Moses could bare and still exist, for afterwards Moses made haste and bowed his head toward the earth.

Your Glory

During a day of prayer and visitation, my heart longed to see His glory. "God teach me your ways." "Let me see your face, show me your glory." I wanted to see His face and to know all there was to know about Him. As I paced up and down the hall, crying, grasping for breath and grabbing my heart I asked God to show Himself to me. "Oh God, I want to know all there is to know about you." I didn't think that was too much to ask after all He wants us to be close to Him and to learn of Him. Well, after my encounter with God and the revelation and vision I received from the Holy Spirit that day, I changed my prayer request to; "Lord teach me your ways, write your words in my heart and guide my footsteps in the pathway of righteousness." Why the sudden change? What happened you ask? Well, it was something so absolutely wonderful, yet startling and fearful (in reverence to God).

After praying, as I laid crossways my bed meditating and yearning to be in the presence of Almighty God, I received my answer. With my eyes closed I saw a vision, darkness like I'd never seen before, and in the darkness were thousands of brilliant tiny particles.

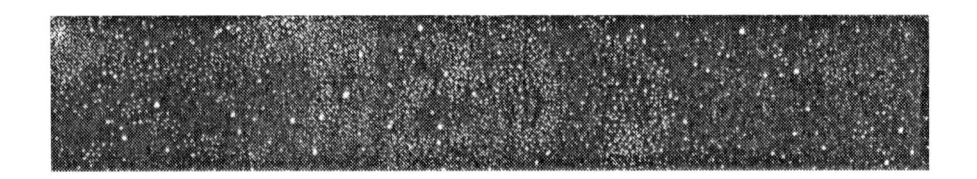

The Holy Spirit spoke to me, "Your flesh couldn't stand to be in my presence. You would explode into billions of particles, like dust in the air. Compare my face to a large flawless diamond with its' many facets. Highly valued and of great substance."

The facets in a diamond are numerous and are used to determine the quality of the stone.

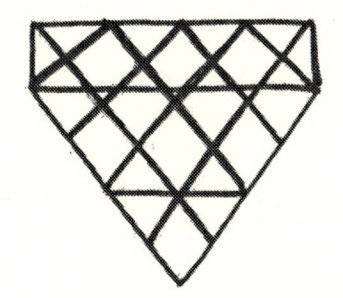

"Thou canst not see my face; for there shall no man see me and live (Ex. 33:20). As I hid Moses in the cliff so I must shield you from me." Our bodies are temporal and cannot exist in the total presence of Almighty God. God shows Himself to us to the degree we can receive and comprehend without being endangered. Our mortal bodies could not live through it.

Mans downfall in the Garden of Eden stripped him of the glory of God (covering) he once wore. He was created in the image of God in his likeness, clothing and countenance, the very essence of God. He wore Gods cloak but exchanged it for fig leaves. Oh, thank God he didn't wear it long. When we are born again we put on Jesus. He is our covering, and we take on a new appearance. Therefore if any man is in Christ, he is a new creature: old things are passed away, behold, all things are become new (II Cor. 5:17).

Moses got a peek of whom God was and was not content with just a taste he wanted more. Because of who God is, he couldn't withstand/comprehend all of God. Behold there is a place by me and you shall stand on that rock. While my glory pass by I will put thee in a cliff of the rock and I will take away my hand and thou shall see my back parts: but my face shall not be seen (Ex 33:21-23).

His Backside

Gods' backside is his after affects, the residuals of the finish product, merciful, gracious, longsuffering, abundant in goodness and truth, forgiving iniquity, transgression and sin. The extent of these characteristics being revealed in our lives is based on our ability to perceive and receive but none of us are able to comprehend it all. We determine how much of Gods' glory, His word (goodness manifested in our lives), He can reveal to us. But when Jesus returns we will become like Him and see Him as He is. The closer we draw to Him the more of Himself He reveals. If you want to see the goodness of God get in His word, spend time in prayer and ask Him to reveal Himself.

Hide Not Thy Face

What is it about His face? More than words will ever know; the purest of pure, bright and out shining any morning sun. No man hath seen God at any time; the only begotten Son, which is in the bosom of the Father, He hath declared Him (John 1:18). Ones' face denotes his relationship/state of mind. Because of sin God turned His face from us less we be consumed. He could no longer look upon man the way He once did, the exact image of Himself, after his downfall in the Garden of Eden. Our visage and relationship changed. We were no longer whole: pure, clean, and godly. We had become sons of darkness, thereby forfeiting our position, and God given right to walk with our Creator and Friend face to face.

Moses longed for and knew the significance of God's face toward him and not from him: the fullness of joy and peace forever more. "How I long to see Him, to look upon His face", an old song still being song today, is a longing for that ultimate contact. The Lord will make His face to shine upon us, and be gracious unto us: The Lord lift up His countenance upon us and give us peace (Num. 6:25,26). For the Lord God will help me; therefore shall I not be confounded: I have set my face like a flint (stone) upon Him, and I know that I shall not be ashamed (Is. 50:7).

> When thou say, seek ye my face
>
> My heart said unto thee, thy face, Lord will I seek.
>
> Hide not thy face far from me:
>
> Thou hast been my help.
>
> Leave me not, neither forsake me

O God of my salvation (Ps. 27:8-9).

The face of the Lord is against them that do evil (1 Pt. 3:12b). "I will set my face against you and you shall be slain before your enemies (Lev. 20:3)".

On This Rock (Christ Jesus) I Stand

Jesus is the rock to the New Testament church: that cliff in the rock where we abide. He that dwells in the secret place (JESUS) of the Most High shall abide under the shadow of the Almighty (Ps. 91:1). Sure and unshakeable is our Lord. The knowledge and understanding of His ways allows us to weather life storms. The life Jesus gave to us and so wants us to enjoy is hidden for us in a secret place in Himself. He hid it for us so that those desiring Him would search for Him with all our heart and then will He be found, says the Lord. He came that we might have life and have it more abundantly (John 10:10).

Removing His hand represents the renting of the veil, allowing access to the Holy of Holies, the mercy seat of Christ. Before the crucifixion only the high priest could go beyond the veil to offer atonement for the sins of the people. Jesus is our high priest and sacrificial offering, through Him we are clothed in righteousness; having access to the mercy seat of God the Father, we can stand boldly before the throne of grace with our petitions. When do we stand boldly before Him? When we have perfected our praise and worship for Him, as revealed to me by the Holy Spirit during worship service, "I don't come down there to you, you must come up here; enter my presence with your praise, and my glory will manifest in the service. Stop waiting on me to come to you, come and get me."

He came to the Israelites, and the Old Testament saints as a cloud by day, pillar of fire by night, burning bush and etc. because they didn't have direct access (the blood) to the throne of grace; Jesus bridged the gap between heaven and hell. God is saying to us "Come here to me, and make a joyful noise unto the Lord, enter His gates with a heart of thanksgiving, and His courts with the tongue of praise, be thankful unto Him and praise His holy name." We in a sense must feel our spirits being translated from earth to heaven during our praise and worship; see and feel ourselves in His presence.

Gods' Glory Illuminated

The heavens declare the glory of God and the firmament shows His handy work. Day unto day utter speech, and night unto night shows knowledge (Ps. 19:1-2). The Gentiles shall see thy righteousness, all kings thy glory: thou shall be a crown of glory in the hand of the Lord and a royal diadem in the hand of thy God (Is. 62:2-3).

Jesus prayed in the 17th chapter of John, "Father, the time has come. Glorify your Son that your Son may glorify you by completing the work you gave me to do. I have revealed you to those whom you gave me and they have obeyed your word. Glory has come to me through them." Does your daily life bring joy to God who invited you into His kingdom to share His glory (good works)? Our light should so shine among men that they will see our good work which gives glory to our Father in heaven.

August 1996, I attended the Southwest Believers Convention in Ft Worth, TX. The praise service was so awesome that we didn't get any further. The glory of the Lord appeared as a cloud of mist throughout the arena, "Because the Lord descended upon it in fire (Mt Sinai was altogether a smoke Ex. 19:18). The house was filled with a cloud, even the house of the Lord: for the glory of the Lord had filled the house of God (II Chronicles 5:13c, 14b)". This was also the evening after I had received the gift of speaking in tongues; no doubt the biggest turning point in my Christian walk, and the night I saw myself, in the spirit, writing a check for 1 million dollars to sow into the ministry.

I saw His "Shakannah" glory on me one morning after having spent the night before wrestling with Him. I was so caught up in the spirit that I finally had to say, Okay Lord I'm tired, I have to get some sleep. The next morning while dressing, I looked into the mirror and thought, how pretty my skin looked. I always had problems with my complexion so this was unusual for me. There was a glow about my face. "Thy face shall be radiant." When Moses came down from Mt Sinai, after spending 40 days and nights with the Father, the children of Israel saw that his face did shine and Moses put a veil upon his face until he was done talking to them (Ex 34:29-33)."

Once, after praying for my sister, Gwinda, who suffers from migraine headaches, I entered the room where she was and saw a bright covering on her face and a beautiful glow about her head. The Holy Spirit spoke to me "The pain is gone but she's afraid to move for fear of it returning." Still other times, as I look back over my life, God spoke to me or revealed Himself to me by His Spirit but I didn't recognize Him. Before, I would call it instinct, intuition or just luck. I couldn't discern His voice. What did I miss?

Brenda A. Peacock

The Peace Of God

"9-1-1 as we refer to that tragic event that shook the Christian body for a moment, this nation for a spell, and the entire world for a split second, left many people terrified and insecure. We never thought or imagined such a tragedy could ever happen in our country. The world looked to our armed forces to avenge the attack on the World Trade Center but God was calling the church to the front line. We sought comfort (minds not our hearts) from the true comforter; The God of Peace for a while, but as time passed, so our thoughts of Him turned away again, and it was back to business as usual.

Many men have searched for a solution to peace, never thinking to sit at the feet of omniscient God. Peace I leave with you my peace I give unto you: not as the world gives, give I unto you (John 14:27), for I will keep him in perfect peace whose mind is stayed on thee (Is. 26:3). Peace is a state of tranquility: freedom from civil destruction, a feeling of security or order as defined by Webster, but it seems to be a rare almost impossible commodity. As we reflect back over the 20th century, there has been little if any peace. Instead we've had wars, scandal in the White House, corruption among government officials and church leaders, murders in our schools, in our homes, and the list goes on. While this chaos is taking place, the church sits watching and often indulging it self.

We are living in perilous times but conflict and turmoil isn't new. Since the fall in the Garden of Eden there has been opposition; one Light (Jesus) who gives us life, joy, and peace in the Holy Ghost: the other darkness (Satan) who offers death, sorrow, and war. November 12, 2001, two months after that devastating attack I was in prayer when a friend called to see if I heard about the airplane crash that day. After I turned on the TV and saw what had happened I began to pray and opened my bible (Isaiah 33:18), "Thine heart shall meditate terror. Where is he that counted the towers?" Coincidence? I don't think so.

With all that's happening around us we need to consider what time it is. Am I ready to meet my maker? What does the future hold? Lord, am I doing those things that are pleasing in your sight? Instead we're asking how can these things be happening to us? Why would God allow it, after all this is the United States? I Thank God that this country was founded and built on the principle that, "In God we trust," by men who understood that without Him they could do nothing but with Him all things were possible. Our forefathers believed in God and prayed for direction, blessing and protection of this nation forever and ever.

Our freedom from God has lead to free...dom...dom from one end of the spectrum to the other (the extreme). How did we get here? What happened to America? I can remember when being an American meant something. We had pride in our work, lifestyle and beliefs. There was pride in the name, but what's in the name now? We have gotten so caught up in the American dream and we spend every waking moment chasing that dream. We have gone about establishing our own plans and forgotten the plans of God.

Answer Me

My people! Hear me. Hear the sound of my voice (my words) as they echo through the walls of despair. Why won't you answer me?
I reach for you through the thickness of the darkest night.
But you will not surrender.
The stillness of the dark encamps you.
That strong fortress of pride, lust, immorality and self- indulgence has gotten the best of you.
You're headed for destruction.
You can't possibly see your way through.
Many evil forces make up the density of night darkness.
No doubt, you need light.
Yet, you continue to struggle with the forces.
One over the others you stumble and fall.
Not in search of the light but running further into the night.
Won't you let me help you?
You see I am the Light.

We must put away our selfish thoughts, ways, and deeds; get cleaned up, wash the dirty laundry, throw out that holy than thou attitude, peel off the skin of self-righteousness, put far from us ungodly thoughts and communication, and crucify our flesh to worldly ways. The gods of this world blind those who fail to follow the light. For God, who commanded the light to shine out of darkness, will shine in our hearts to give the light of the knowledge of the glory of God.

Jehovah Shalom, the God of Peace, promised peace always by all means (2 Th. 3:16); wholeness in our spirit, soul, and body: complete and perfect (mature) creatures like unto Him, but unto

the wicked there is no peace (Is. 48:22). We won't fear the attacks of the enemy because we have the blessing of God (Mt. 5:3-11) in and on our life: happiness and favor with God and man; it doesn't just happen, it is granted to us. Blessings come from a heart living in pursuit of the character of God, and no time has it been more crucial for us to pursue His character and righteousness than now. The Lord will bless His people with peace (Ps. 29:11).

Brenda A. Peacock

When I Feel Lonely

> There is a place in God that only I can fill.
> Only I can make home there.
> He'll only share with me, will only tell me, and only say to me.
> I'll be the one He whispers to concerning this matter.
> Yes, I am special and so are you.

There have been times in every believer's life when you just wanted God to love on you just because, to feel Him in your midst? Those are the really special times. You're not in a crisis situation; you're not in need of anything but His love. God loves those moments, not that He frowns on others, but just like you and I, He wants us to want him for who He is (His face) and not what He has (His hand). Matthew 6:33 instruct us to, seek the kingdom of God first and all these things will be added.

I arrived home early from work one afternoon. I felt the presence of God and just wanted to spend time meditating and loving on Him. As I sat down and rested my head on the back of the loveseat, I drifted into a light sleep. It was during that time that I saw myself resting on Jesus' shoulder, all cuddled like a baby. I felt so relaxed, peaceful and secure. There is rest in Him, and He gives us a sweet peaceful sleep. When I awakened I remembered the story of Lazarus how after his death he went to rest in Abraham's bosom

Rest my soul
When you're tired, burdened, or feel so alone.

No friend, family, or love one, seem to be home.

There is no one to talk to, so what do you do?

Jesus is the answer and He will

see you thru.

An out of body experience

I stated earlier, I moved to Dallas but I didn't tell you that I got there by way of Lake Jackson, TX. That was my first home away from home. I was dealing with some things that had burdened me down. I had joined a very nice church in Freeport, TX. It was there during Sunday morning service that again, I felt His awesome comfort as my spirit literally left my physical body.

During praise service I began to weep and cry out to God, "Lord I'm tired and I don't know what to do." As I lifted my hands surrendering my cares to God, my spirit left my body and was suspended in midair. Literally, I was in the spirit looking down at my physical body. Talk about a high that was a high. Yes that's the feeling it left me with, an out of this world high. I've never experimented with drugs, thank the Lord, but I guarantee none can do you like Jesus. Of course, it happened so fast, but it was incredible non the less.

He has the whole world in His hand

The earth is the Lords' and the fullness there of, them and they that dwell there in. Stop and think, how could God know all, see all and be everywhere at all times? Sure God is bigger than life, He measured the waters in His hand and blew win with His nostrils, but God I need your help with this. My finite mind can't comprehend how you can be all places at once, know all things and be all things to all people. I was perplexed and began to seek Him for answers. I know you're saying that's what makes Him God but that wasn't enough for me. I needed to understand.

I had envisioned Him sitting in heaven looking down on us, and while that may be true that wasn't the vision I received. Or should I say, He showed me a vision that gave me peace. I saw in my dream the arms of a beautiful fiery gold throne, and sitting on the throne were two person's dressed in robes that stopped right at the floor, and the color of their robes were the whitest of white. And the Ancient of Days did sit, whose garment was white as snow, and the hair of His head like the pure wool: His throne was like the fiery flame (Daniel 7:9).

As I observed, one had in His lap a clear globe, which He watched over so lovingly. No I did not see a, head, hand, hair, or face, no man can see Gods' face and live. The only thing visible to me was the arm of the throne, the white robe draped to the floor and the globe, all of which I perceived to be The Father and Son watching over their creation. It may not seem much to you but it was just what I needed. I have such peace now. I no longer wonder how, I just know that it is.

"May I Have This Dance?"

There is therefore now no condemnation to those in Christ Jesus, who walk not after the flesh, but after the Spirit (Rm. 8:1). I've spent the majority of my Christian walk focusing on the "restrictions" placed on a believer rather than the "liberty" that was given me: the dos and don'ts of Christianity. The adversary in many areas still holds us captive, but one encounter with the Holy Spirit will change your life forever. My change happened this past summer, while attending my 30th year high school reunion, when I agreed to dance with a classmate.

As innocent as it might seem to many, I spent the rest of the night in condemnation. I was confused, still holding on to the idea that my actions determine my eternal outcome rather than the assurance that, my salvation was given to me by the grace of God and is irrevocable. There is no force, person or event powerful enough to take me out of the hands of the Father. This revelation didn't come over night. It took Jesus as my dance partner to make me realize He is a God of fun, laughter, and good times; In His presence is the fullness of joy and at His right hand are pleasures forever more (PS. 37:11).

During Sunday morning worship, I closed my eyes and saw myself in the spirit dancing with Jesus. We were alone, just He and I, in what appeared to be open space. He held my hand and turned about as I danced, danced, danced all around Him; and they began to be merry (play music and dance). A few weeks later

I attended a women's seminar and during worship, I began to cry out, "Lord I want to dance with you," as I closed my eyes and began spinning around, I saw beautiful streams of light circling around me.

Jesus entertains and wants to be entertained; after all we were made for His good pleasure. Ecclesiastes 3:4, there is a time and purpose for everything under the sun including dancing. David, a man after Gods' own heart loved to dance before God, and Jesus' first miracle was performed at a marriage feast where they were drinking and making merry. Hear me, I'm not an advocate of worldly pleasures, the point is this; Satan can no longer condemn me, I will not be held captive by his ploy to keep me sin focused. From this day on I will stand fast in the liberty wherewith Christ hath made me free (Gal. 5:1) because if/when I fall down He'll pick me up.

Brenda A. Peacock

My Warring Angel

This story begins with an event that happened February 12, 2001. I met an angel in human form. Be not forgetful to entertain strangers: thereby some have entertained angels unaware (Heb. 13:2). Of course I didn't know she was an angel but I knew there was something spectacular about her. Prior to our meeting, my relationship with God left a lot to be desired but afterwards, my life would never be the same. The transition occurred over night but the effect will be long lasting.

I was a member of Grace Community Church in Texarkana, Texas at the time, and as part of our outreach ministry we had invited Ms. Hammond, I referred to her as "My Michelle," a powerful and anointed woman of God to conduct a seminar on how to develop a love life. I was appointed as her personal attendant, while I wasn't keen on the idea or excited about the seminar initially, I accepted the assignment. I had formed my opinion of the entire event and thought I knew the content: seeking God for your mate and dating. Boy was I wrong; instead I was about to embark in an event that would change my life forever.

The closer it got to the day of her arrival a spirit of expectation came upon me. I began to feel in my spirit that God had something special for me, unless you've experienced that feeling;

With My Whole Heart

it's hard to explain. I began a three day fast asking God to open my heart and allow me to receive a double portion of whatever He had for me. The big day finally arrived. Sister Knight and I met Ms Michelle at the airport and took her to get a bite to eat before going to the hotel. From the moment I saw her I knew there was something different about her, calm, gentle, yet firm. When she walked it was as though her feet never touched the ground (glide), and putting on her coat was like watching someone in slow motion (not limited or controlled by gravity); it appeared to take forever yet it only took a second.

The first night of the seminar, "Get A Love Life," wasn't anything like I expected: dating and our relationship with one another. The seminar centered on how to develop an intimate and loving relationship with God. She taught us how to read and view the bible from a totally different perspective, one of romance and of people having relationships and interacting with God. To actually feel what Abraham, Enoch, David and other patriarchs felt: real people experiencing real life situations and their personal encounters with The Creator. Imagine Adam walking and talking with God. Enoch being so close and intimate with Him that one day God took him up. And there's Moses, who saw God so close up that afterwards no man could look upon his face.

The bible is a book about real people and true relationships. Reading my bible now has taken on a whole new dimension: I read expecting to feel God's presence, hear His voice and see His hand at work. God wants us to learn of Him through the study of His word in order that we might understand and comprehend with all saints what are the breath, length, depth, and height of His love for us. The seminar was explosive and food for the soul. I'm certain that most if not everyone received a blessing by attending but with certainty she came specifically for me. She had to make an impartation and yes I believe I received.

I mentioned earlier that I asked God for a double portion of whatever He had for me, right? Aren't you curious to know what it was and whether I received it? The answer is Yes! Yes! Yes! The seminar went from Friday night thru Sunday afternoon. The first night of the conference I returned home a little after midnight, still full of the spirit and weeping continuously. The love this woman had for God I now desired and I knew God wanted me to have it. That night I knelt by my bed and prayed, "As Elisha and Elijah Lord let me receive the mantle and a double portion."

Elijah was a great prophet and a fiery man of God who went up by a whirlwind into heaven but prior to his departure he asked his companion and successor, Elisha, "Ask what I shall do for thee, before I be taken away." Elisha, "I pray thee, let a double portion of thy spirit be upon me." As Elijah ascended up Elisha took up the mantle that fell from him (Elijah). The mantle was a loose cloak, covering, and represents the spirit (anointing) in which Elijah operated. As Elisha received from Elijah I too received from my Michelle the mantle and a double portion of the spirit of love that was on her.

I saw in a dream that night a large black piece of cloth wavering or floating above my face. It wasn't touching me but it covered my entire view. I awakened the next morning overwhelmed by my experience.

Oh how I love Jesus, because He first loved me; the words to a song I learned as a child but did not understand until I began to mature in my Christian walk. It's not just a song; it is an awesome revelation of the key element in our relationship with God, His perfect and undying love for you and I. The message that God loves me more than this world will ever know has finally reached my soul and embedded in my heart.

The anointing that removes burdens, destroys yokes, and delivers us form the fiery darts of the enemy is found in the knowledge and understanding of God's love for us. The seminar lasted three days and too much my surprise extremely low in attendance, none of the members of the church where the seminar was held attended; our sanctuary was very small and we hoped for a large turn out. Why God, I asked, and His response, "Pastor Knight made it available, they didn't reject him they rejected me." God always over extends Himself. Unfortunately people willing accept the invitation but fail to attend the banquet (Lk. 14:16-24). Those who were in attendance ate from the masters' table.

Brenda A. Peacock

I Lack Nothing

Money is a very touchy subject so let's go ahead and get it out of the way. After all, most Christians don't believe God is concerned with supplying their every need much less giving them the desires of their heart. We feel so sanctimonious and holy when we are broke, busted and disgusted, because then God sees me suffering for the cause. What cause? What can you possibly do for the kingdom when you, yourself, suffer lack? And the thought, a Christian having a nice bankroll, why, that's ungodly.

My people err, not knowing the scriptures, or the power of God (Mt 22:29). You ask, and receive not, because you ask for the wrong reasons, that you may consume it upon your lusts (Jas 4:3). Money answers all things (Ecclesiastes 10:19b), but seek first the kingdom of God and his righteousness and all these things (bought with money) will be added (Matthew 6:30). They that seek the Lord shall not want any good thing (Ps 34:10b). How then can we be justified in our traditional thinking?

We have to change our way of thinking and see ourselves as God sees us: whole, nothing missing nothing broken, and lacking absolutely no good thing. God wants us overflowing in wealth and our spirit man consumed with His presence. I've purposed that I will have all that God has promised me in His word, therefore I can say with assurance that my inheritance is astronomical. I

don't have room for it all so I'll have to give it away. I actually saw myself, in the spirit, writing a check to a Christian ministry for 1 million dollars. I am a distribution center for the kingdom. I give for the furtherance of the gospel, aide to children, help the needy, and feed the hungry souls.

The gospel must be preached throughout the world and God needs you and I to do it. It's not enough to have money; you must know what to do with it when it comes (mission). Thou shall remember the Lord thy God: for it is He that gives the power to get wealth that He may <u>establish His covenant</u> that He swore unto thy fathers (Deut. 8:18). You see God wants to prosper us for kingdom work, but not all of us are mature enough to handle the increase. We have to be committed and willing to let Him lead us, to not love the money and the things it can buy rather than obeying Him. If therefore, ye have not been faithful in the unrighteous mammon (riches of this world), who will commit to your trust the <u>true riches</u> (Luke 16:11)?

While driving home from church one night, God spoke to me, "I can trust you with the <u>true riches</u>." I began searching the word for revelation on <u>"the true richest"</u> and found in Rm 11:33, "O the depth of the riches both of the wisdom and knowledge of God! How unsearchable are His judgments, and His ways past finding out!" The <u>true riches</u> are the wisdom and knowledge of God. Who better knew the value of such a treasure than King Solomon, when after building the temple, was asked by God, "Ask what I shall give thee." Solomon responded, "I am but a little child: I know not how to go out or come in. Give therefore thy servant an understanding heart to judge thy people, that I may discern between good and bad." The speech so pleased the Lord that He gave him according to his word, a wise and understanding heart, and things he did not ask for, both riches, and honor and long life (1Kings 4:5-14).

Church, know there is a wealth transfer that has already taken place in the spirit realm and God is positioning and equipping His people to receive it when it manifest in the natural. He's waiting on us to come into the full knowledge of Him as Jehovah Sabbath,

(The Lord of Host) our commander in chief. Get ready no demon in hell can stop it.

As I look over my life I have allowed Satan to steal so much from me due to my lack of Knowledge of who I am in Christ and understanding of our "Salvation package" purchased on Calvary. I'm getting my stuff back. The kingdom of heaven suffers violence and the violent take it by force (Mt 11:12). The kingdom of God is within me and all I need is found in the presence of God for, in thy presence is fullness of joy; at thy right hand there are pleasures forever more (Ps 16:11). Yes He did it all for me and I receive all that is mine.

His Hand Extended Out

Several years ago I desired a new car, a pearl one to be exact. I saw my car in a dream, only it wasn't pearl it was black. I awoke shaking my head, and immediately spoke, "Lord I don't want a black one". Well approximately two years later I was driving a new car, black of course. But that wasn't the vision, it came after I got the car. I had begun praying and seeking Gods' word concerning finances, specifically increase and debt cancellation on my house and car note. I'd heard the word of God in these areas and begun to understand and believe that God desires His children to have things in abundance. You know we get what we ask for. Well, I saw a vision that was so real and starling.

There appeared, in the cherubim's, the form of a man's hand under their wings (Ezekiel 10:8), and I looked, behold, a hand was sent unto me: and lo, a roll of a book (envelope) was therein (Ezekiel 2:9).

He put forth the form of a hand (Ezekiel 8:3). Behold, I send an Angel before thee, to keep thee in the way, and to bring thee into the place that I have prepared and to prosper thy way (Exodus 23:20, Gen 24:40).

And I received the letter from the hand of the messenger (II Kings 19:14a). That is correct. August 1998 as I sat meditating in prayer, with my eyes closed, there appeared flashing across my face, a hand extending down from heaven. In the hand was a white envelope (the exact size, shape and color of my mortgage statement) being transferred to what I perceived as an angels' wing.

That huge feathery wing flapped so close to my face I jerked back to avoid being hit, that's how close and real it was. The Cheri

bums' wing was whiter than snow, feathery and fluffy like a beautiful dove, and that right hand extended out (strong and high is thy right hand, exalted and doeth valiantly Ps 89:13b, 118:16), absolutely breath taking. God sends His angels before us to prosper our way. Later He said, "You shall see angels ascending and descending." No, all things have not yet manifested for me in the natural, but I've seen and received them in my spirit. Amen.

What does that vision have to do with increase or debt cancellation? Like Daniel, I believe the moment I prayed, God answered me. From the first day that thou didst set thine heart to understand, and to chasten thyself before thy God, thy words were heard, and I am come for thy words (Daniel 10:12). He opened His hand, and satisfied my desire (Ps 145:16). I will give thee the treasures of darkness, and hidden riches of secret places, that thou may know that I, the Lord, which call thee by thy name, am the God of Israel (Isaiah 45:3). God has cancelled all my debts because I desired it of Him (Mt 18:32).

He is putting His people in position for the wealth transfer, just as He did Israel prior to their exodus from Egypt, for the wealth of the wicked is laid up for the just. Thou have caused men to ride over our heads; we went through fire and through water: but thou brought us out into a wealthy place (Ps. 66:12). He's looking and waiting on us, His bride, the Church, without a spot, wrinkle or blemish to take our position: possessing and operating in the authority given us.

Abide With Me

What a privilege to be alive. Nothing compares to the gift of life. Every single moment should be lived to its fullest. Without life there is nothing. Life has a purpose and I was purposed in and for life.

God in His infinite wisdom created me for a purpose. Predestined my life and strategically mapped out my highway of life, the route I would take no doubt. I admit I've taken detours, ventured from the trail more times than I care to mention. I've driven down many side roads and many one-way streets. Whenever I take a notion to go my on right a way, and not the right-way (seek of Him a right way Ezra 8:21), I find myself traveling on a dead end street.

God is not far from us. He is very near us in our hearts and minds. Christmas 1998 I had a visitation from the Father. I knew this would be a Christmas to remember. For several weeks, as I sat studying the word, I would have a feeling of someone coming to my door. On numerous occasions a spirit of fear would come over me, a fear of someone knocking at my door. I couldn't understand, "Why would they knock and not ring the doorbell?"

I left work Christmas Eve with such excitement. I planned to spend the entire day seeking God. When I arose Christmas morning the Holy Spirit spoke to me, "Get dressed you are going to have company." I thought, no one is coming over here, and if they do, surely they will call first. I proceeded to take care of a few things then I sat in my comfortable chair with my trusty sword in hand and believed I would hear a word from the Lord.

As I began to read, the anointing came on me and I began to pray in the spirit. Suddenly, I heard a loud knock that initially startled me. Instantly, I realized it was not the door to my house but the doorpost of my heart (spirit), and the Father speaking thru His word, "<u>I stand at the door and knock if any man will answer I will come in and supp.</u>" The knock sounded so real, and I felt overwhelmed that God considered me. He was visiting with me. Everything was happening so fast. I wept with tears of joy and excitement. I never imagined in my wildest dreams that I would have a visitation of such magnitude.

My Walk In The Spirit

Picture this a beautiful hill site, green pasture, still water and a gentle breeze. He makes me to lay down in green pastures, leads me besides the still waters, restores my soul and leads me in the path of righteousness for His names sake (Psalms 23).

With My Whole Heart

I dreamt of a beautiful pasture with blades of grass so green and perfect in shape (sharp and erect), height was a little below my knees and every blade the same size. Underneath the grass laid water, not quite covering my feet, to be exact it was right at my ankle. As I went through the grass, I didn't appear to be walking or riding, more like gliding across, I could see the water lying beneath me, crystal clear and undisturbed. The most amazing thing was how still the water laid and how quickly the grass sprang back, as though it had not been touched.

My friend Beverly suggested I got a glimpse of heaven. I didn't know what the dream meant but I knew that I had never seen grass so beautiful nor spring back so quickly without leaving an imprint. I also knew that the Holy Spirit would give me revelation of my dream and He did, on July 5, 2001, during my time of study, "And he brought me through the waters; the waters were to the ankles, representing the walk of the believer in the spirit" (Ezekiel 47:3). We must learn to walk in the spirit and not after the lust of the flesh.

Our Christian walk is based on our maturity in Christ. As our bodies go through stages of development: infant to toddler, child, teen, into adulthood, so our spirit man must be nurtured and allowed to grow and mature in Christ Jesus. Our bloodline is of royal priesthood, Jesus being our High Priest. God fashioned us in His likeness and because He is a spirit we too are spirit beings. We are journeying through a foreign country: our final destination is heaven above. We travel by way of our spirit man with the Holy Spirit guiding and directing our every step.

Our level of commitment determines our growth. We can be content with just knowing what we have and never obtaining it or we can accept our God given inheritance and begin living it right here and right now. I don't know about you but I'm not complacent. I won't stop until I'm swimming (prepared for service) in that water (Holy Spirit). It's not enough for me to walk through the water. I have to be trained to swim (prepared for service), for the creek will rise first to the knees (prayer), then overflow into the river.

Brenda A. Peacock

Burning Bush

Our Father is concerned with every aspect of our lives, big and small. Imagine Him showing you how to wear makeup. In a dream God spoke to me "only the eyes and lips." Why, because I asked Him. I have sensitive skin and always had problems wearing it. Or going house hunting and He says, "This is what I have for you my child." From the time we awake, all during the day and through out the night He's perfecting all that concerns us. Yes, He is interested in the simplest little thing like the makeup we wear but above all is His interest in our spiritual maturity.

One day as I meditated on the word concerning the prophet Moses and his first encounter with God, I was caught up in the Spirit. As I felt His love and how He commissioned us to go out and preach the gospel He began to speak, "Moses encountered me as a <u>burning bush</u> that was not consumed. You are now that <u>burning bush</u> because the Holy Spirit lives inside you." A year later during praise and worship, as I closed my eyes I saw what appeared to be fire permeating from my body. I was on fire but not being consumed.

I saw as the color of amber, the appearance of fire round about within it, from the appearance of His loins even upward, and from the appearance of His loins even downward, I saw as it were the appearance of fire, and it had brightness round about. This was the appearance of the likeness of the glory of the Lord (Ek. 1:27-28).

Oh!!!!! What a brilliant yellow-red array it gave, like flames from a burning fire. Who makes His angels' spirits, and His ministers a flame of fire (Heb 1:7)? It was an awesome experience. We are to be on fire for God and the Holy Spirit is that fire from which we receive power to raise the dead, lay hands on the sick, trample on serpents, eat any deadly thing without harm and be victorious in our Christian walk (Mark 16:17-21).

How does one abide in Him and what are the benefits? According to Webster abiding means to remain steadfast, faithful, and continue in a certain condition. King David wrote in the 91st Psalms, He that <u>dwells</u> in the secret place of the Most High shall <u>abide</u> under the shadow of the Almighty. That secret place is in the Lord Jesus Christ. We dwell (permanently reside) in Him when we understand and accept His undying love for us thereby rendering our whole heart, soul, mind, and body to Him and Him only do we serve. Because I set my love upon Him and made Him my refuge and my habitation I'm assured that He will deliver me from the evil. He shall cover me with His feathers and under His wings will I trust: His truth (word) shall be my shield and buckler. I am set on high because I know His name.

His name is above all others; being the brightness of Gods' glory and the express image of His person, was made so much better than the angels and obtained a more excellent name than they. The power of His name, the name of Jesus, and the power we have by use of His name. It's in His name; all power is in that name. I am set on high because I know His name. When I understand my legal right to use His name I can call on the name of Jesus and know that He will answer: He will be with me in trouble; deliver me, and honor me. With long life will He satisfy me and show me His salvation.

We have peace when we learn to walk and abide in Gods' presence; take on His countenance. He becomes our refuge and our habitation: our dwelling is the secret place of the Most High God.

Brenda A. Peacock

His Face

Marriage, the first institution established by God ordaining the union of man and woman to replenish the earth, has become nothing more than a social event: you dress up, invite guest, eat, drink and have a gala time. When the party is over, and the guest are gone, there's nothing left but the check. Most couples aren't finished paying for the wedding before they've added another expense, the divorce. Of course some factored that in the cost. What happened to that saying, it's cheaper to keep her? Better yet, what about their vow for better or worst, for richer or poorer, and keep me only unto you?

I'm speaking to you women, especially those of you who desperately want a husband but can never find "Mr. Right!!!!!!" because "he's all wrong." We're not taught to seek God concerning our mate or how to hear God about our mate. Who knows me better or knows what's best for me but God? It is not good that the man should be alone; I will make him a meet (Gen 2:18). Seek ye out of the book of the Lord and read: no one of these shall fail, none shall want her mate: for my mouth it hath commanded, and His Spirit it shall gathered them (Is 34:16).

In 1997 God told me I would marry and later revealed him to me in a dream, not his facial or physical makeup but his spirit. As we were standing facing one another I said, "I love you" and was about to ask him, "Do you love me," when I looked into his face and knew in my spirit the answer. I nodded my head as I spoke with assurance, "I know, I know," then turned and walked away. I'll know by his spirit before I see him in the natural: this man will be a judge (Is. 33:22), a man in whom the Spirit of God is, a mighty man of wealth (nothing missing).

December 1999 God instructed me to, "Be prepared, all dressed and ready for my wedding feast (Luke 12:35)," and what's a bride without her gown? That's right I purchased a gown, mine you, no mate in sight. Of course this isn't something you willingly share with people, definitely not the normal process but I share it now because of what happened later: I did marry but not like you think. The first store I entered, and the first dress I tried on I bought. I knew immediately it was for me: fabric (100% silk), color (off white), down to the texture (like linen). The original price was $999.00 on sale for $99.00. What a bargain but more important was what God said as I left the store, "You will live off the 10% and give 90% of your increase," that was just the beginning.

It wasn't the most gorgeous dress ever but something happened whenever I put it on: an awesome glow round about me. One afternoon as I woke from a nap, I saw a silhouette of a bride carrying her bouquet on my wall; I knew in my spirit it was I, God spoke, "I am your husband," My Maker is my husband (Is. 54:5). When I receive a visitation of such magnitude I'm reminded of how special I am to Him; not in comparison to anyone else but based on my own personal relationship with Him. How is God my husband and am I ready to be a wife? Since the fall of man in the Garden of Eden God said to the woman, "Thy desire shall be to thy husband;" a desire that he can't fill. That security, satisfaction, fulfillment, and heavenly covering adorning the first Adam no longer exist in fallen man.

Adam was given charge to provide protection, comfort, security, support, intimacy and etc. to his helpmeet but fell short. We still seek those things but its God and God alone who can fulfill us. Before He gives us to marry He desires to be our husband: to have a heart for Him, desire Him (intimate), put Him first, depend on Him only and be whole and complete in Him. When we can receive Him as our husband: provider (gown), nurturer (strength), and manager of all earthly affairs, He will join us to our helpmeet, someone liken unto Himself (same qualities).

God was now my husband but could I be the wife He desired of me? Was I willing to separate myself from the world to be and do whatever He commands? Not yet. But as time passed I underwent major pruning in preparation for my husband: learning submission by humbling to Gods' authority in and over my life, obedience to His word (always in my best interest), temperance, self-control (etc.), and a willingness to accept the person God has for me; the latter being the most difficult. Why? Because I was convinced I knew what I wanted in a mate. I know how to choose my mate, I thought, but I erred not knowing the scripture, and I had my own ideas about marriage: expecting more from him and not willing to give much of myself. I wasn't aware I was in such a mess until God began to work in me. He never leaves us like He finds us. He's constantly molding and shaping us into that perfect bride without a spot or wrinkle.

I had not totally surrendered to Gods' will concerning my mate. I felt the love my husband will have for me; liken unto the love of God, which means he will not abuse me, or take advantage of me but he will look out for my best interest. What more could a girl ask for? My willingness to accept that person meant not allowing my own inhibitions or society to limit God. I stated earlier I would know my husband before I saw him. But what I didn't tell you was I assumed, no questions asked, that he was black (why an issue)? I honestly didn't know and couldn't see that I was walking in darkness, being blinded by the color of ones skin (prejudice), yet professing to be a born again, spirit filled Christian; am I talking to any of you?

I'm not against interracial dating or marriage; I once like this guy (white) but I wouldn't go out with him, "what would people say." It's easy to blame others, besides it's my preference. No big deal or was it? Is color an issue with you? Would you object to (skin color) who's coming to dinner? God has no tolerance for self-pride or prejudice, both extreme and opposite ends of the spectrum. He revealed this unclean spirit (bias) in my heart through dreams; three to be exact: I was walking alone when out of the blue a man (white) appeared and began walking beside me; in the second dream two men (white) approached me on one side and a man (black) on the other, again I walk away with the two men (white).

I was quite disturbed by the dreams and sought God for understanding. I also shared them with my friend Beverly whose response was, "you have to be open minded, don't limit God." I didn't want to hear that because I was opened minded <u>when it came to others</u> but as for me, God didn't want that for me. That was not my desire and God gives us the desire in our heart (Ps 37:4). How is that for twisting the word to make it fit? The scripture actually reads "Delight (high regard or rapor) yourself in the Lord then He will give you the desires of your heart. When we take pleasure in the things of God He will show us a better and perfect way.

The third dream was as I described earlier; my husband to be and I were facing one another and I knew he loved me but what I didn't tell you was that I perceived him to be black so I knew God and I were on the same page. But I couldn't dismiss the other dreams. I continued to question God and it didn't take Him long to answer. I was in Wal-Mart early one Saturday morning when a white lady walked passed me pushing her baby (biracial) in a buggy; the Holy Spirit immediately spoke, "<u>White women have the right idea</u> (unbiased love)", openly embracing the union between the races and apparently understand that it's not about color, status, society, or such but a matter of the heart). That one statement revolutionized my thinking.

I heard a story of a young boy (Caucasian) who was watching a boxing match when his father entered the room and asked who was winning? "The one in the red," the child answered. His father was startled by his response because the most obvious or noticeable difference wasn't their shorts but their skin: one was

Brenda A. Peacock

black and the other white. What that child saw were two men who's shorts were different in color; innocence at its purest (the mouth of babes). But what happens to us? Why does growing up cloud our minds and harden our hearts to diversity? Why can't we embrace the differences in one another? God does, doesn't He?

God will bring our darkness to light. He will uncover and expose your heart; spew out the impurities, mend the brokenness and restore wholeness in equipping us for service. He rid me of that ungodly stronghold: that bias attitude hindering His plan. My mate and I will be equally yoked, rooted and grounded in the word. God is not a respecter of persons and we must see others and ourselves as He sees us. We are engrafted into His body and there is no color barrier/difference in the body of Christ. In a marriage the two shall become one, no you and me but us, great or small but equal, no black and white but a beautiful blend. This wasn't just about marriage, black or white, but about Gods people walking in love and loving. What a tragedy to allow the flesh to hinder our receiving from God. I can't love God and discriminate? It's not His character. Seeing, loving, and accepting a person for who they are inwardly is the Christian way.

But Will He Love Me?

Fantasize being in love. What would it be like? I will love him/her but will he/she love me? I received my answer to that question, and actually felt it as I awakened one morning with an overwhelming feeling of love.

I saw in a dream the head (no facial features) of a man, odd complexion with thick-black curly hair, lean his head beneath my breast.

As his head touched my chest I felt this incredible transfer of love; it was such a powerful and overwhelming sensation that I was awakened. Because God had been dealing with me concerning my husband, I had no doubt that was the purpose of the dream. I felt in my heart and spirit that I'd heard from God concerning my husband so I responded, "Oh God, I know, my husband will love me like you."

I saw his hair, but there was something about that hair, men don't wear their hair like that anymore: big thick curls, different from an Afro or curl and jet-black. Then there was his complexion. I didn't see his face or any other features other than his skin tone, not black or white. I was puzzled; there was something about his hair and complexion. It would be 3-4 months latter before I received revelation of this dream and the magnitude of my experience.

It was Father's day weekend (2001). I was on the computer and watching TBN, a Christian television station. The program was a documentary/study on what Jesus would have looked like; His facial features, hair and etc. They were describing His features: hair texture (wooly), skin color (olive), facial structure, and stature. Glimpsing the TV, my spirit quickened as this image appeared. That's what I couldn't describe, His wooly hair and olive complexion. Coincidence? I don't think so. I knew immediately who the person was in my dream. It was Jesus. My beloved one is tanned and handsome, and He has wavy, raven hair (Solomon 5:10). No doubt it was Jesus resting His head in my chest and depositing His love in my heart. He's after your heart, to change it from stone to flesh.

A Heart For God

The heart is the organ that pumps blood (life) throughout the body, thereby the seat of physical life, the center of moral, intellectual, and spiritual life. When the bible makes reference to the heart (the very center of a man) it refers to the latter, the spirit of a man. When we are born into this world (of corruptible seed) our spirit is sin infested. We must go through a rebirthing process in order to have the heart/spirit cleansed. The very nature of a man's heart is enmity to God. God is holy and righteous and in Him is no sin.

The condition of our heart is crucial to our walk with God. Man looks at the outward appearance, physical characteristics and intellectual aptitude in determining ones status but God looks at the heart. He searches to and froe throughout the earth seeking those who have committed themselves to knowing and following Him. Guard your heart with all diligence for out of it flows the issues of life.

He Hurts Too

We hurt God when we grieve the Holy Spirit; deny His existence in and over our lives, refuse to surrender to His authority and when we allow the evil one to reap havoc in our lives. God hurts and we inflict the pain.

He allowed me to feel His hurt through a couple behaving in a manner that offended Him. The Holy Spirit spoke to me, "He hurt me." It hurt God because she was now a part of him (the two become as one) and a husband is to love his wife. I began to weep inwardly as my heart was heavy with grief, unlike anything I'd experienced. I could barely contain myself. I felt God's pain, and He unction me to tell the young man how his behavior offended Him, and to instruct him to "Love his wife." I wanted to be sure I was hearing from God, after all I didn't feel that it was my business.

"God, if you want me to say something then let him approach me." Well sure enough, after the service was over, the young man turned and came strait to me. I began to weep as I told him what God had placed in my heart; how his actions hurt God, that God wants him to love his wife, and that he would never be whole without her. He was very receptive and told me a few days later how God had been dealing with him all week and proceeded to thank me.

That same night as I was returning home I asked God why did He allow me to experience that? His response, "<u>You have a heart for me.</u>" He then brought to my remembrance King David, a man after Gods' on heart. And I will give them a heart to know me, that I am the Lord: and they shall be my people, and I will be their God: for they shall return unto me with their whole heart (Jr. 27:7).

On yet another occasion while attending a social event, I saw an old friend whom I'd not seen in over 25 yrs. We spoke cordially, and he proceeded to say, not to me but to the others standing by, "She should have been my wife." Why would he say that? Some may think it was flattering, but mind you, he was already on his second marriage and my heart went out to her. She was all I could think about. She's with someone who doesn't love her, and not because he loves me, I'm certain of that. Apparently she was not his wife, without a doubt he is not who God has for me, and one has to ask, "Is he <u>the person</u> God had for her?"

The most painful of all was when God said, "we (saints) pimp Him," play around with Him; toiling with His affections. We seek Him but swear He can't be found, call on Him and fear He won't hear, pray unto Him but doubt He'll answer. We are prone to give up, give in, and sell Him out at the slightest conflict. We don't take God or our place in Him serious. We have a form of godliness but no substance; like a pimp we expect all kind of favors from Him. I am broken with their whorish heart, which hath departed from me, and with their eyes, which go a-whoring after their idols.

What does He owe us? Nothing. What has He giving us? Everything. He is constantly reaching out to us desiring that we take hold of Him. Hear God and be in tune with His Spirit. I'm not walking in excellence with Christ but this I can be sure of, "His hand will lead me and His right hand will hold me," (Ps. 139:10). I have purposed in my heart that nothing will stop me from reaching my predestined place in Christ Jesus.

Oh! What happened with the dress you ask? Well years have passed, and I've out grown it, but I continue to study, follow, and rely on my heavenly Father who is my first husband, to lead me into the things of God.

Brenda A. Peacock

An Ear to Hear

How can God be so intimate and make me feel so special? He gives me so much attention. He feels my every waking moment with His presence. He's never far away and I'm never alone.

How can you love me so? This world will never know. What are you in search of? All we'll ever need is found in the person of Jehovah!!!

>Touch me with your ever presence,
>>Whisper sweet words in essence.
>
>>The echo of your mighty voice,
>>Sends waives of laughter throughout the course.
>
>>My heart panders when you approach,
>>Mindful and fearful of your reproach.
>
>>I know that sound,
>>It is familiar,
>>Please won't you come nearer?

We are a chosen generation and God has chosen us for a specific purpose. Thou Lord, who knows the hearts of all men, show

With My Whole Heart

whether of these two you have chosen. That he may take part of this ministry and apostleship, from which Judas by transgression fell that he may go to his own place (Acts 2:24-25).

God is looking for men and women who have a heart for Him. Isaiah heard the voice of the Lord say, "Who shall I send, and who will go for us?" "Then said I, Here am I; send me (Is. 6:8)." Can you answer as Isaiah did?

Saturday morning, August 1996 I was instructed to literally enter my closet and pray. After spending about an hour in the presence of God, I returned to bed only to be redirected to get my bible and return to my closet. In obedience to God, I got my bible, returned to my closet and waited to hear from God. When I opened my bible it fell to Exodus 34:10 behold, before all thy people I will do marvels which has not been done in all the earth or in any nation and the people among which thou art shall see the work of the Lord, for it is a terrible thing that I do with thee.

I cried out to God as the Holy Spirit moved in my heart. God was speaking to me. He had a plan for me. He was going to use me. What an awesome experience that was. I had no idea where that would lead me, or what God was going to do in my life, but I've never let go of that prophecy. As God was speaking to Moses concerning Israel in those days, He is now speaking to the church. Now, after three years, a battle with depression, family turmoil, and all that Satan could do to try and stop me, I can now count it all joy, for behold God has begun to perform those things spoken to me of from the Lord (Lk 1:99).

June 7, 2000, I answered God's call on my life. I was in prayer that morning when I began to speak, "I press toward the mark of prize of the <u>high calling</u>." I began to weep and cried out, "I'll do it, whatever you want me to do, I'll do it." I fell to my knees before the Father, crying and praising God as I confessed my willingness to surrender to Him. I got up and sat on the sofa only to have the Holy Spirit instruct me to go get my bible. Of course I obeyed. I was going to turn to that scripture (Phil. 3:14)) when the Holy Spirit brought to my memory the vision I had that night, a

Brenda A. Peacock

bible opened and nothing legible but the number at the top of the page, 143.

I opened my bible to that page and began reading verse 29-30; the holy garments of Aaron shall be his sons' when he cometh into the tabernacle of the congregation to minister in the holy place. I was sure that I had heard from God, and I know that the gifts and calling of God are without repentance (Rm. 11:29). I have an assignment and He is equipping me for the job.

There's more, I had a second dream and again a bible was opened. I saw two words on the page one was underneath and adjacent the other.

The Holy Spirit asked me twice (in my dream) if I could pronounce them. I nodded yes as I pronounced the words, Lo-de-bar and Ma-ha-z-ai. I was familiar with the word Lo-de-bar and it's interpretation, (a place, a lowly state of being), but I wasn't familiar with the second word. I searched the bible and found Lo-de-bar (1 Sam. 9:5), underneath and a little adjacent to it was Me-phib-o-sheth (read the story). Me-phib-o-sheth was Jonathan's son, sole survivor, and grandson of Saul the first king of Israel.

With My Whole Heart

Fleeing from the hands of then king David, he took refuge in Lo-de-bar.

God was telling me there would be a change, I will show thee kindness and restore thee and you shall eat at my table as one of the King's son (1 Sam. 9:7,11b). Now I hear you saying, how could He be talking to you? Is. 62:2 states when God calls you He also gives you a new name, could Ma-ha-zai be my new name? I wouldn't be the first, (Gen. 12:1,17:1,5,15) God changed Abram and Sarai's name to Abraham and Sarah, and Jacob's name to Israel (Gen. 32:23-28). The Gentiles shall see thy righteousness, and all kings thy glory: and thou shall be called by a new name, which the mouth of the Lord shall name (Is. 62-2).

I will plant you (by the rivers of water)

August 2001 was yet another turn in my Christian journey. It began a few weeks prior to this Sunday I'm writing about. I was not aware of what God was about to do in my life but as I look back things had already begun to change. I taught the young children's Sunday school. Saturday night arrived and I was not prepared for class. I decided I would arise early Sunday morning and study so off to bed I went. But guess what? The Holy Spirit would not let me rest, so I got out of bed and began to studying my Sunday school lesson which was taken from the book of Joshua 3:5.

As I began to read, "sanctify yourselves for tomorrow the Lord will do wonders among you", I new God was speaking directly to me, something was going to happen Sunday but I didn't know what. I arose that Sunday morning, got dressed, and arrived at church early. My spirit was not at ease during class time. I felt a nudge to leave a few times, but I dared not, after all I was teaching. I had forgotten the scripture I had read the night before. Later, during praise and worship, I had this feeling that, "I have to go", so I grabbed my purse and walked out the door.

Before I got to my car the Holy Spirit told me I would be joining Pastor Tracy's church. I had never seen or heard this pastor before nor did I know where it was located. No, I've never been there before. How is that for blind faith and being lead by the Spirit? A friend planted the seed several months prior to this event. She invited me to visit this church with her but I didn't go.

I was determined to hear from God that day. I didn't go to Pastor's Tracy's church that morning; I didn't know where it was. I drove to my friend's house, she told me where the church was but informed me that service started at 10:00. It was almost 11:00 a.m. by now and I didn't want to step in church an hour after the service was to begin so I decided to go somewhere else. As I entered the church the pastor was beginning to read the text (Philippians 1:6), Being confident of this very thing, He who hath begun a good work in you will perform it until the day of Jesus Christ. I knew God was confirming his word and getting me in position to carry out His plan.

After service, I returned home, fell on my face before the Lord to seek confirmation that I did in fact hear Him. As I began to pray God told me again I would join that church. I asked, "why that church?" His response, "I'm going to plant you," and from that moment on I was at peace. I hadn't heard that phrase, "<u>Plant you</u>," nor did I remember having read it before. I asked God the meaning and where, if at all, it was in the bible. When God tells us things he confirms it with his word.

Nov 27, 2001 while in prayer and meditation, I opened my bible to Jeremiah 42:10, I will plant you and not pluck you up. King David also recorded in Psalms 1:3 "He shall be like a tree planted by the rivers of water. I'm presently planted and flourishing as a member of <u>The Family Word Church</u> in Texarkana, Texas; the place where God sent me. God placed me here in order to prepare me for the most difficult time of my life, the home going of my mom.

The Transformation

I will always remember the years 2000 and 2001. I reached a major milestone in my walk with God during this time. I encountered circumstances, no different from others, but the key was the lessons learned. My faith took on a new dimension. I went from hoping and praying that God would answer, to knowing he already had, and standing on his word until the thing I believed Him for manifested.

It all started with my undergoing major surgery. I was diagnosed having fibroid tumors and was beginning to feel some discomfort. I opt to have surgery, which was the turning point in my walk with Jehovah. Several of my friends had gone thru this and it wasn't a big deal, so I thought. Approximately 3 months before this I learned that two of my cousins were having the same problems. The Lord spoke to me, "Satan is attacking my daughters where the seed is nurtured and birth takes place." I recalled the scripture in Gen 3:15 "I will put enmity between thee and the woman, and thy seed and her seed; it shall bruise thy head and thou shall bruise his head." I did not know that God was preparing me for my own personal battle with the adversary.

In March, I had surgery and everything went well. The tumors were not malignant, of course. I hadn't entertained the possibility of cancer. The idea never entered my mind. I remember the doctor telling me the results of the lab and at that moment I thought, "hum wonder why I had not thought about the possibility of my having cancer?" Again, everything was normal; nothing out of the ordinary except the day I had the staples removed.

Your typical office visit, I arrived on time, the wait was short and off to have the usual vital signs checked. Then into the room, I go, undressing and mounting the table like a turtle in extra slow motion. The incision appeared to be healing normally but as the nurse begun to remove the staples a small area opened. The doctor came in; looked at the scar and asked if I had anyone with me. My aunt Wilma had accompanied me and would remain with me throughout the week. She was summoned to the room and informed that the opening of the incision, the size of an eraser head at the time, need to be cleaned daily. He then took a q-tip dabbed it in peroxide and began cleaning the opening.

Well, as if that wasn't enough, the lower part of my stomach began to open. Things were really moving fast now. The doctor, with both hands, immediately pressed down on my stomach and began to tare the womb open. All I could do was press the sides of my stomach together, squirming, and wanting desperately to draw my legs in a fetal position. I could hear or feel it tearing apart, like material separating at the seam. I had never experienced anything like that in all my life. I didn't have time to catch my breath. What seemed like eternity only lasted a few seconds. My mind thought and first response was to cry out, "Lord why me," but before I could open my mouth the Holy Spirit spoke, "Why not you?" I immediately repented for having thought this should not be happening to me and cried out, "Lord have mercy!" "Have mercy Lord."

Time stood still, yet it all happened instantly. How could all this conversation take lace in such a short time? I don't know, but it did. God is not bound by time one day is as a thousand years and a thousand years as one day. You see God does not operate in time. He made time for us. In addition, the Lord did show mercy.

The healing process was not normal or pleasant. I used a wet to dry application in which gauze soaked in peroxide was packed in the womb 2 to 3 times daily (approximately 2-3 inches deep) and allowed to dry. It was very painful removing the dry gauze from this raw area and the air hitting the deep opening in the dead of winter was an unforgettable experience. I am going somewhere with this just stay with me. Healing from the inside out and not outside in was the revelation I would learn and I can't think of a better way to have had it taught. God deals with us; teaches us and observes us, from our inner man not our outward appearance. He searches the earth seeking those that have a heart for Him. Having a renewed mind was the lesson to be learned.

What started out as six weeks leave of absence turned into nine weeks and still my womb was not completely healed. My doctor's visit, each week, was always a challenge. The prior night I spent toiling over the idea of not healing properly. I would awaken early in the morning consumed with doubt and worry that it was not closing the way the doctor said. He assured me that I would not be able to tell the difference. But I tell you, I thought, "That doctor must be crazy, there is no way this thing is going to close all the way. Look how thicker the right side is compared to the left. And look how wide apart it is." I couldn't see how the two sides would fuse together, no way. "He should be able to look at it and tell this isn't right. Why is he lying to me when he can see himself it's impossible. If this were his wife, he would do something about it. He wouldn't want her looking like this. There's going to be a trench in the middle of my stomach."

This conversation went on every week and during these conversations and prayers, I would quote scriptures, one in particular, "Speak those things that be not as though they were." I tried to keep focused, but I knew what I saw, and what I saw was not good. I won't tell you how angry I was but strangely, the Holy Spirit would not let me say anything. I occasionally questioned the doctor and sought assurance that everything would be okay. Sure enough it didn't close the way I hoped. Instead it closed just like I thought, spoke, and saw in the natural.

The morning prior to my last checkup, I awakened early to pray. I mentioned before that during my prayer time, I would pray that my stomach would heal properly but that morning I didn't think about my stomach. I returned to bed and began meditating, when the Holy Spirit began to speak, "You're the reason it didn't heal the way it should have. The doctor said it was going to close but you said it couldn't. You kept looking at the natural (flesh), and not the spiritual realm. If you had just caught on to what the doctor was saying, speaking those things that are not as though they were, but you didn't believe it. He kept telling you it would heal but you kept looking with your natural eyes. You don't operate by this world system but in the spiritual realm. Be not conformed to this world but be ye transformed by the renewing of your mind that you may prove what is that good, acceptable and perfect will of God (Romans 12:2)."

All I could do was repent and cry out to him for forgiveness, "I didn't know. I thought I knew, I thought I understood." I thank God to this day that my incision didn't close properly and rejoice over all that happened. It was a lesson well taught and worth the price. Learning to operate in the spirit world requires a new mode of thinking. The kingdom of God (doing things God way) is at hand. It is necessary in order to overcome the battles of this life, "For we war not against flesh and blood but against principalities against powers against rulers of the darkness of this world against spiritual wickedness in high places."

Renewing Your Mind

A renewed mind was the focal point throughout the course. When your mind is in line with Gods' word faith will immerse. Having faith that does not waiver will move any mountain. God in His infinite wisdom has given us a sound mind, the mind of Christ. How we choose to cultivate, fertilize and nurture determines the crop it yields. Don't misunderstand, I don't profess to have all the answers or to have perfected this but I do have a working knowledge of what we have in Jesus and I've begun to build on that revelation.

With My Whole Heart

As Jesus was transformed on the Mt Of Transfiguration we to must be transformed by the renewing of our minds. We must take off the old man (sin nature) and put on the new; the righteousness of God in Christ Jesus, letting this mind be in us that was also in Christ Jesus. Jesus was born of a woman but of an incorruptible seed, the Holy Spirit. He had no sin nature because His bloodline was Jehovah God. Jesus was God in the form of man but while on earth He operated not as God but as a man. He had to past the test that Adam failed in the Garden of Eden in order to redeem mankind. He had to overcome the adversary, Satan, not as God but as a fallen man.

The first confrontation, which would determine the ultimate outcome, is recorded in Matthew 4:1-11, Jesus being lead up of the Spirit into the wilderness to be tempted of the devil. Satan, the tempter, appeared three times and "<u>takes Him up.</u>" Did Satan literally take Him or did He willingly go? I don't believe Jesus would willingly go anywhere with the devil and I'm positive Satan couldn't take Him against His will. So what actually took place? How did the devil appear to Jesus? Was it in the form of a serpent as in the garden, an angel or some other beast? Just what did happened?

Jesus said, "The things I do even greater you will do because I go to my Father. You won't be tempted anymore than I. Speak the word, resist the devil and he will flea, and (Eph. 4:27) give no place to the devil." Remember, Jesus came not only to die for us but also to teach us how to stand against the enemy. We can't be lead by Satan and go places he suggest or wants to take us. I believe the battle took place in the arena of the mind where Satan launched his attack against the first Adam and succeeded in obtaining authority and dominion over this world. But God had a counter attack, a plan to "<u>beat him at his own game.</u>"

The devil appeared to Jesus in the arena of His mind and attempted to place thoughts that were contrary to those of God. Jesus immediately renewed His thinking by speaking <u>the word</u>. Jesus, a man anointed and empowered by the Holy Spirit, defeated Satan in the arena of the mind with <u>the word</u>, ultimately regaining man's rightful ownership in God's creation. He took back what Satan gained illegally from the first Adam. This same process of speaking God's word raised Jesus from the dead. Jesus confessed the word that was prophesied thousands of years before His birth. He was the Messiah, the one who would be crucified, lay in a tomb three days, and arises with all power in heaven and on earth. Because He spoke the word, the anointing that was in Him was alive and performing those things spoken to Him of by the Father.

Yet Another Attack

Over the past several years I've had encounters no different and possibly less devastating than a lot of you. I've had financial struggles, lost of love ones, two within a week's time, my brother-in-law and my mom in May 2002 and attacks on my body, the most recent of which I would like to share with you.

March 2002 I noticed this small bump on my left hand. As it began to enlarge, it leaked of a clear fluid, and resembled a boil. I was home helping with my mother at the time the first one came to head. I was asked several times if possibly a spider had bitten me. Well approximately 2 weeks later a second bump appeared. Bypassing all the graphics, when it was all over I had ten boils to appear on my body within a period of seven months.

After the second bump was almost cleared and number three was in the making I decided to seek help. I prayed that God would lead me to a doctor who would know what the problem was and could treat me. God instructed me to see Dr Scott Wyrick, a local dermatologist, who upon first glance, described the symptoms, diagnosed it being "Furunculous," a bacteria infection that attacks the hair follicles of the skin. Supposedly there is no cure for this disease.

Although Dr Wyricks' diagnoses and treatment was correct in the natural, I didn't receive that report in my spirit. Yes I took the medicine and did all I was told to do until 10/28/02 exactly one hour shy of being five months after my mom departed this life. What happened on that day? Well, I hope you know that there is

<u>**The Great Physician**</u> whose name is Jesus and by His stripes I'm healed (Is 54:10). I was working on boil number nine and ten; they were now coming in pairs.

At approximately 4:00 a.m. on 10/28/02 I awakened after seeing a vision of a finger pointing directly at me, and a soft sweet voice saying,

"Those bumps will not come upon you again."

I knew immediately who was speaking to me. I began thanking God and rejoicing over my victory for I had received a word from the Lord.

Three weeks later my friend Beverly called my job but I didn't get back to her until later that afternoon. Guess what? The timing was perfect. The presence of God was heavy that day and when I did speak to her she confirmed what I had been feeling, that God was doing a mighty thing in my life. I could tell in her voice that something was up. She told me that I had been on her mind that morning and God spoke to her, "Brenda, a present day Job, Satan has attacked her finances, love ones (mom), and those boils on her body. Tell her like Job I will return to her 100 times what the enemy has taken from her because she has been faithful."

> **Father, because I know your love for me, my life will never be the same. You have touched me in ways I never dreamed possible. Thank you for the awesome deposit you made in me, the Holy Spirit, and for the perfect sacrificial offering, Jesus Christ the Lamb of God, who paid my sin debt in full. Satan we serve you notice this day that we will have what we say and the gates of hell shall not prevail against us. You have no power or authority to lord over our lives because we live in accordance with the word of God in Jesus name. Amen, and Amen.**

It was six months ago that I saw His hand. Later I was attacked with 2 more boils because I continued to live in fear and worry of their returning instead of trusting Gods' word and having faith in His love for me but I didn't react with fear, take another pill or make a doctor's visit; instead I asked God what was the lesson to be learned? The answer was to stay focused on Him not my circumstance, grab hold of the word and take a firm stand against the adversary.

The problem is we don't have a strong foundation (wisdom, knowledge and understanding) to hold us up when we're faced with a trial. It's hard to walk in victory when you're constantly being defeated, so what are we to do? How can we be and do all that God has commanded? The answer recorded in Gen, 11:6, the people had begun building a tower to reach heaven, the Lord came down to see and said, "Behold, the people is one and one language, now <u>nothing</u> will be <u>restrained</u> from them which they have <u>imagined</u> to do. Then in Mk. 11:23 Jesus said whosoever says and believes, not doubt, he shall have whatsoever he say. It's called the <u>battle of the mind.</u>

Most of us think that if we are to be victorious God has to act, move on our behalf, but on the cross Jesus' declared it was finished, took His seat at the right hand of the Father, and is now interceding for us. His work is finished and He's seated in heaven waiting on the body (church) to work with the mind (Christ Jesus). God has delivered us and given us a new way/birth but He is hurting, hurting for his children because they don't understand the bloodline.

When I Need You Most

I mentioned earlier the attacks on my body and the revelation I received that we make Gods' word of non affect with our tongue and unbelief: looking at the natural instead of the spiritual, speaking those things that be not as though they were and not being conformed to this world but be transformed by the renewing of our minds. Those teachings were in preparation for a much greater challenge that involved the life/death of someone very close and dear to me, my mom. It would no doubt be the battle of all battles due to what was at stake.

It was the best of times yet to some the worst ever. A time when I needed God more than ever before and He was there. Tuesday, May 28, 2002 my mom made a choice to depart her temporal life on earth and enter her permanent resting place: a choice that would take her throughout eternity. I never imagined her not being here with me. I miss her, wonder what she's doing, and often ask, "mom what is it like, what are you learning and how does it look?" Yes, I would love to hear her voice, see her smile, and taste her delicious sweet potato pies (the best in the world), but I don't wish her back because I know where she is. Why would I want her to leave a safe haven and return to a world of chaos? I wouldn't come back would you?

Letting her go wasn't difficult but understand why required personal and uninterrupted time with the Lord. I spent countless hours rehearsing the events leading up to that day, wanting to understand why, how, now what, and time on my face before Him inquiring of His will concerning sickness, disease, and premature death. Sure, we will all make that journey, if the Lord tarries, but the way we depart in route to our final destination left me with unanswered questions. So I asked questions, and while receiving some answers the reality is, there is so much more that I won't ever know. God showed and revealed a lot throughout my moms' illness, and that which I comprehended helped to make her home going a joyous one.

Divine Set Up

"I will tell you of things to come before they happen. I don't keep any thing hidden from you. Ask me of the things to come concerning my sons, and concerning the work of my hands. I have not spoken in secret, in a dark place of the earth: I said not unto the seed of Jacob, seek me in vain (Is. 45:11,19)." The Lord had spoken to me concerning my ministry; the things He would do through me. On this particular night, as I was returning home from Wednesday night service, He began speaking to me about raising the dead. He had spoken this to me before but this time it was different I asked a question, "Who, who is it," and He answered; "Your mom," not in an audible voice but in my spirit by the Holy Spirit who is the teacher, instructor and ear of the all omniscience God. I didn't like the response, had trouble acknowledging that it came from Him, and questioned Him, "Why would and how could this be so?"

That was a hard pill to swallow. I began to rebuke Satan and tried to put it out of my mind by saying, our mind does play tricks on us, and attributing it to the enemy, trying to put worry and fear in my heart. God's reply to my question would enter my mind periodically, but I would shirk it off. In less than a year I would need that same word from God as assurance, to give me faith, hope and trust that if He has purposed it so shall it stand, and if

He has spoken it so shall it come to pass. Why didn't I heed the warning and take action to circumvent the enemy's attack.

A Word From Above

My mom first began to complain of unusual stomach discomfort and occasional pains in the lower abdomen approximately two months before we knew the seriousness of her illness. She visited her gynecologist who began treating her for kidney disorder. Finally she went to her family doctor whom she all but swore by, who ran a few tests, had suspicions and referred her to a specialist. Mom didn't tell us what the doctor suspected but when she was scheduled to see the specialist I went home to be with her; unaware of the specialist field of medicine.

On the morning of her appointment I arose early and got on my face to seek God about her illness. I asked God another question, "What is it: what's wrong with my mom?" and His response, "An infirmity." I immediately got up, got my bible, and preceded to search for scriptures on infirmities in order to combat the evil that had raised its ugly head. I then shared with my mom the word I received from the Lord and the scriptures.

God's Promise

Ps 77:10 This is my infirmity: but I will remember the right hand of the Most High (length of days is in His right hand Pro. 4:20).
Pr 18:14 The spirit of a man will sustain his infirmity: but a wounded spirit who can bear?
Mt 8:17 Himself took our infirmity, and bares our sicknesses,
Lk 5:15 Great multitudes came together to hear, and to be healed by Him of their infirmities.
Lk 7:21 And in that self same hour He cured many of their infirmities and plagues, and of evil spirits: and unto many that were blind He gave sight.
Lk 13:11,12 There was a woman who had a spirit of infirmity, and when Jesus saw her, He called her to Him, and said unto her, woman thou art loosed from thine infirmity.

Ro 6:19 I spake after the manner of man because of the infirmity of your flesh; for as you yielded your members servants to uncleanness and to iniquity unto iniquity: even so now yield your members servants to righteousness unto holiness.

Ro 8:26 Likewise the Spirit also helpeth our infirmities; for we know not what we should pray for, as we ought; but the Spirit itself maketh intercession for us with groanings, which cannot be uttered.

Ro 15:1 We then that are strong ought to bare the infirmities of the weak, and not to please ourselves.

Rev 22:1,2 Water of life: And He showed me a pure river of water of life, clear as crystal, proceeding out of the throne of God and of the Lamb. In the midst of the street of it, and on either side of the river, was there the tree of life, which bare 12 manners of fruits, and yielded her fruit every month. And the leaves of the tree were for the healing of the nations.

Two weeks after the surgery an angel visited my mom: a tall, slim woman, wearing a beige suit, hair cut in a pageboy style about shoulder length (moms' description). The angel called out to her, "My infirmity," mom answered and sat strait up in bed.

My Infirmity

To my grandmother, and the Angel that healed her

An Angel rolled the stone away
An Angel said "My Infirmity"

She came to me in a dream
Knowing my every need

Two words she only spoke
Reality told me I was woke

Her look said, "I am here for you"
"Your name has been reproved"

"Oh no, you're not through"
"Revived again, reborn are you"

"A new level is awaiting"
"Child you've been made brand new"

She took the sickness that I had
The weapon that could not prosper

Healed from head to toe
My temple, my testimony

Her wings spread apart

Brenda A. Peacock

> Her lips departed to speak
>
> Two wings flowed very peacefully
> "My Infirmity"

Crenisha Mone't Wright
Copyright ©2003 *Crenisha Mone't Wright*

In Times Like These

My sister, aunt, and I accompanied my mom to the specialist in Memphis, Tennessee. Upon arrival we located his office, got her checked in and waited patiently for the doctor: still unaware of his profession. After a short time she was called back; I accompanied her into the patient room, and within minutes the doctor entered, introduced himself and his field of medicine, oncology. I tell you anger (not fear) rose up in my spirit and my inward response was, "Okay devil (not the doctor) you have declared war."

The doctor said based on all the reports and test it appears she had ovarian cancer and recommended surgery immediately. He went on to inform her of the prognosis (1-3yrs) with that form of cancer. He was a Christian, thank God, so I shared what God had spoken to me and He joined with our faith and the word that mom would be healed. I thank God He called it an infirmity, thereby keeping fear at a distance, and not allowing the enemy to plant that seed of death that's associated with the slightest mention of cancer. However, I learned later that my moms' primary doctor, the one that made the referral, told her he suspected it was cancer but she didn't mention it to us. I also believe that from the minute she heard that word she was in fear.

The fight had begun and we were not going down by default, so I thought. Satan wins by default when we operate out of worry and fear because he knows, unlike most saints, that God has already sent His word, healed them, and delivered them from their destruction. We would live in worry and fear of the outcome for sometime to come. I finally admitted I was afraid and took it to God. It was Wednesday night and I was headed for church, when

With My Whole Heart

I stopped and made the confession, "Lord I have a spirit of fear on me. I know it didn't come from you because you didn't give us a spirit of fear but of power, love, and a sound mind. You have to take it from me because I can't get rid of it on my own." Afterwards I felt a relief, and that night Pastor Knights' sermon was on <u>**FEAR**</u>, "False Evidence Appearing Real." Coincidence? No, not hardly. I received a little knowledge but no revelation. That came months later as I matured in my understanding of the Fathers' love (conquers all), which freed me from that spirit of fear.

I had a dream about moms going for a checkup, she was trying to tell me something the doctor said but I wouldn't let her, I told her, "I don't want to hear it. What does the word say? That's all I want to hear. I'm not receiving anything else and I'm not going to listen to anything else." I refused to listen to her and I knew that was the enemy trying to deliver bad news and put fear and doubt in my mind. Later, the Holy Spirit told me, "Like Job the very thing she feared has come upon her," and mom continued to live in fear until the end.

My grandmother and aunt, her mom and older sister, both died of cancer several years prior, she cared for them during their illness so all she knew was what she saw happen to them. She believed, and I've heard her say, "We all have to die with something," and "God knows best." She had already put her tongue against God's will and ability to heal her; according to thy faith be it unto you. The wrong seed was planted and deeply rooted in her heart. I tried to help her dispel those old myths, mindsets, teachings (or like of), and get her mind in line with God's word so faith could do its perfect work.

Back to the surgery, it was approximately two weeks after the diagnosis that she had the first operation; time was of essence. The report wasn't good; she required chemotherapy, a second operation, chemo and still a third one due to a bowel obstruction. After the second operation she later told me she started not to have it because she was feeling so good, and believed God had healed her. At the time there was no sign that the disease had come back, it was done in case they didn't get it all. She wasn't taking any chances, which makes me wonder if she really believed.

It was a long grueling ordeal but we grew in the Lord. The most difficult thing for me initially was the chemotherapy. The day she had the first treatment, I walked into my office, pressed my face against the wall and prayed, "That <u>the eyes (mind) of my understanding be enlightened that I might know the hope of His calling</u>," (Eph. 1:18). My mother, and His child, was attacked. I wanted to understand how and why this was happening. What could I do to get God to heal her? As I meditated on that passage, even to this day, I'm learning that He has done all He's going to do, the rest is up to us; know that everything works by love, we're to be victorious over our enemy, and have revelation knowledge of God and His plan for us.

Weeping Nights but Joyful Mornings

I returned home a week before her discharge to make preparations to be home with her while she recuperated. It was during that time, Saturday around midnight, while interceding for her, that I received a revelation about sickness and disease. As I began to meditate, no weapon formed against you shall prosper (Is. 54:17), the Holy Spirit said, "What is sickness and disease? A tool or weapon used by the enemy. I didn't say it wouldn't come upon you. I said it should not prosper. If one of mine die due to a sickness or disease then that weapon will have prospered." Lord, what about the disciples? They were beheaded and stoned. "No greater love that a man lay down his life for a friend. They gave their lives for the furtherance of the gospel. No man took my life I gave it. My people perish for like of knowledge."

I had a hold of something, the word on healing. I bought tapes on healing and salvation, and for the first time mom heard the truth. We began to speak the word, claim victory over her situation and hope for her life but when Satan has gained entry and the soil of your heart has not been cultivated it's a struggle to get the word to take root. Satan's lies will go deep if we don't uproot him and stake our claim. That's what happened with my mom, she loved

Jesus but didn't understand her legal right to be healed simply because He loved her. A few days before she went to be with the Lord she asked a question, "What did I do that was so bad?" The countless hours, day and night, she must have laid awake in fear, worry, doubt, and condemnation, allowing the devil to falsely accuse her and rob her of the certainty that the promises of God are yes and Amen.

Deep down she felt it was Gods will for her and He was punishing her for something. Like so many of us she didn't understand the breadth, length, dept, and height of His love for her, otherwise she would have known that He doesn't put evil on His children. But her flesh had gotten weak, grown tired and physically unable to resist. It is at this point when the strong spirit of a man sustains his infirmity but a wounded spirit cannot bear? We can't afford to wait until a life or death situation is beating the door down to strengthen our spirit. We must be on guard, prepared for the attack; the kingdom of heaven suffers violence, and the violent take it by force (Mt. 11:12).

Heaven was prepared for us but not waiting on us. Why die before your time? We have an appointed time but God appoints not every time; it's not always our time when we go. Prolong your days in the land (Deut. 11:9). The apostle Paul's flesh and spirit was in constant war; the flesh wanting to remain to help win souls but his spirit longed to see Jesus; to be absent from the body and present with the Lord. Heaven is home for all who die in the Lord but we are needed here to do kingdom work.

What will happen the moment I see Him? Will He hug me and welcome me with out stretched arms; I always imagined He would. I hope He'll say thou good and faithful servant, and not why have you come so soon. A month or two before my mom went home I had a vision. I saw God sitting behind a huge desk in a large courtroom, His arms were folded and I was standing before Him. As He leaned forward, across the desk, looking down at me, He asked, "Why did you allow the enemy to overcome you? You had everything you needed within you to defeat him (Satan)." There won't be an excuse, God requires us to be victorious in our walk with Him. If we stand our ground we are guaranteed the victory and God is not a respecter of persons. Paul had a choice and chose to stay, we too can choose but either way we will give an answer for the choices we make. It depends on the circumstance, how we leave this life. We choose our destiny in life, which inevitably determines where we will spend eternity and we will all spend eternity somewhere.

My mom and I both gave up the fight. She began preparing for death before she became physically unable to resist. She once said, "If I don't make it don't ya'll worry about me." I assured her that I wouldn't worry because I knew she would be with Jesus. I then shared with her my vision; that if we allow the enemy to overcome us God will ask us why. As for me I gave in when I stopped looking with my spiritual eyes and began noticing her physical state. Taking your eyes off God and focusing on the circumstance all but guarantees a win for the devil.

Her Journey Home

The last few weeks of my mom's life were hard, she was bedridden, had lost a lot of weight and was weak; she couldn't turn over or pull herself up in bed. Although I spent a lot of time with her it wasn't enough. I held her, kissed her, song to her and loved on her. I even slept with her when I was home because I wanted to be there for her, to sit her up if she got strangled or vomited, to turn her over if she got tired of lying in one position, and just because. I wouldn't get much sleep or rest most nights; I heard every grunt or cough, and felt every move she made. I probably worried her by always asking, "Mom, are you okay?"

Monday May 27, 2002, Memorial Day was the last day mom was with us. We were all with her that day and she had other visitors as well. Periodically I would check on her and her guest to make sure everyone was comfortable. Strangely, whenever I entered her room I felt warmth that apparently no one else could feel. I asked time and time again if it was warm to them but they were comfortable. All the other rooms felt nice and cool to me but the minute I stepped into her room I could feel the warmth. I even got up several times that night adjusting the ceiling fan off, on, high

With My Whole Heart

and low trying to get comfortable. I guess that was the first sign but the most unusual event happened that night.

When I was home no one else had to stay but that night my oldest brother Cecil decided to stay as well. I thought I had convinced him to go home but he soon returned saying he felt he needed to stay. He bunked out in the den where he could hear the monitor. There was a child's monitor by her bed so we could hear when no one was in the room with her. Of course I slept with her, and normally I wouldn't get much sleep because I heard every sound she made, but not that night. I had a restful night and the most peaceful sleep, but the Holy Spirit would awaken me periodically to witness with my eyes and ears my moms home going. Cecil witnessed it also; he could hear her through the monitor.

Here she was, a person who didn't have the strength to feed herself yet sat propped up by pillows, arms lifted up, and head bobbing side to side, praising and worshipping the Lord all night long. I was beginning to think she was loosing her mind because she was carrying on so. How could she go on and on like that? My brother came into the room several times during the night to see what was going on. We tried to give her something to calm her down and make her sleep but she wasn't having that, she shook her head, tightened her lips, and refused to take it. Later I tried patting and holding her hand, but she pulled away, shook her head saying, "No baby."

A lot went on in the spirit realm that night; saw her parents and sister who preceded her, received the heavenly language (speaking in tongues), and talked with the Master. I heard her call Him, "Jesus my savior," and my brother heard her say, "Jesus my friend and brother." I know she saw Him; I asked her, "Mom are you talking to Jesus?" but she didn't answer me. Early that morning Cecil came in to check on her before leaving, and we briefly discussed the events of that night. I almost told him then that mom was going home today but I couldn't.

Remember, I said earlier God told me I would raise her from the dead, and later I did ask Him how? His answer, "What is it to you?" Well it was about 4:50a.m when mom began to gag, I still see her frowning and shaking her head in disgust. I hated seeing her go through that almost as much as she hated going, finally I said as I stood over her, "Mom it's okay you go to Jesus." Within minutes she started again, as I raised her up, I noticed she wasn't supporting herself so I sat behind her in bed bracing her limp body. She began spitting up what appeared to be blood; it was dark in the room so I couldn't see that well. Afterwards I laid her back down and upon entering the bathroom detected it was indeed blood. Calmly I called hospice, explained what had transpired that night, and informed her that she was vomiting blood.

I finished the call and went to check on her. I walked over to her bed and had begun to recant my statement, "It's okay you go to Jesus," when I noticed blood on the corner of her mouth. It was over. My mom was gone. My heart was instantly filled with unspeakable joy. I wasn't sad, glad; neither grieved nor relieved but I had the peace of God that passes all understanding. To this day it's hard to believe I accepted/reacted that way. I love my mom and couldn't imagine life without her. I didn't think I could live without her but God prepared my heart. I was with her and witnessed her awesome journey home. I failed my assignment. Yes I raised her up as her heart made it's last beat and she drew her last breath but that wasn't the way I thought or God's perfect plan even though He knew the outcome, the end from the beginning. I know it was not God's perfect will for her to leave here due to that sickness.

I Won't For Get You

I wasn't scheduled to be at my mom's the week she passed but the sudden home going of my brother-in-law Marvin, the Wednesday before brought me home. He and my sister were married for over 20 years and have two wonderful children. Marvin was a quiet person, good father, husband, and a friend to many. The 21 years he was a part of our family we never just talked. Not because we didn't get along, but he was just quiet. All my nephews enjoyed talking to him and my mom would always say, "Isn't that right

Marvin? Marvin knows," seeking his agreement when she was telling my sister something.

Saturday, May 25, 2002, three days before my mom's home going, we were having Marvin's funeral. I went to get in my car and couldn't find my keys. I searched my bags, the house, and suddenly remembered going in the trunk that morning, laying the keys down, and telling myself, "Remember to get the keys before you close the trunk." No that wasn't a smart thing to do but that's what I did and guess what? I closed the trunk with my keys inside. I couldn't believe I had done that, and then I remembered this had only happened to me one other time, 21 years ago. 21 years ago that May, on there wedding day, I locked my keys in the trunk of my car.

Hear me I've locked my keys in my vehicle twice in my driving career, both times in the trunk and both time events associated with my brother-in-law. Is that significant? Yes, because of what happened after I returned from the funeral. I walked around the car checking doors hoping one was unlocked. As I walked back to the house and stepped under the carport I heard Marvin's voice as though he was standing right there say, "Don't forget me sister-in-law," and afterwards his funny chuckle. I stopped in my tracks and said (crying), "O I won't forget you." He was one of a kind, and we truly miss him.

Brenda A. Peacock

The Perfect Man

Dedicated to my daddy……………….Marvin Edward Wright

On that day of May
I didn't know you were going away
Now you're gone
But your memories will always live on
It's so hard now
To cope with the fact that you're gone
But you made us strong
So we're moving on
We will always think of you
Morning, noon, and night
And long for that day
When we can reunite
No more heart ache, no more pain,
No more cloudy days or rain
You are free now, fly away
I know that I will see you again someday
Mark the perfect man
For the end of that man is peace
Perfect peace
Until we meet again

Crenisha Mone't Wright

Copyright ©2003 Crenisha Wright

My Comfort

There is joy in the home going of a saint. Joy and happiness when you know that you know you know they are present with the Lord. I know she's in heaven because God told me so the day before her funeral. The service was just a formality because mom gave herself a home going, and nothing could match it. The family was scheduled to view the remains that Friday afternoon, an hour before, the funeral director, Ms. Effie, the absolute best there is (I wouldn't have trusted my mom with anyone else), called and needed me to come there right then. I wasn't dressed and was in the process of fixing my hair but she insisted she needed me to come right away. I didn't know what was going on, and didn't ask any more questions. My mom's oldest sister Lillie wanted to go with me but after her aunt and my great "aunt Effie" drove up she decided to ride with her, so I went alone.

While driving down the road, I began praying and talking to God, "God, I know you have something to do with this. I don't know what it is but I see your hand in this, and I'm not afraid." Upon arrival I went into her office, sat down and asked what was going on? She looked at me and answered, "I don't know why or what made me do this, I just thought about you all of a sudden. I don't usually do this but I felt you needed some time alone before anyone else got here." Of course I began crying as we stood and walked toward the viewing room.

My mom's brother, "uncle June" as we call him, an employee at the funeral home was already there. I was about to enter the room when he attempted to stop me but Ms. Effie said, "She'll be all right, she needs to do this."

He opened the door, and the second I entered the room, I fell on my knees with my hands extended up in praise because of the glory that hovered over her; a brilliant light like an <u>angel</u>. As the spirit of the Lord fell upon

Brenda A. Peacock

me, He said to me, "I have received unto myself a precious jewel." I began to cry out in tongues as I felt His awesome presence. It was a marvelous experience that made me realize this was not the end but a new beginning, and I know I'll see her again.

Angel in the Midst of Angels

Dedicated to a Glorious Woman, grandma, Virginia Peacock

She walks with grace and beauty
A smile that's brighter than the sun
Her everlasting memories
Shall forever lead us on

Her laughter fills the room with glory
The heavens know her name
To look upon that beautiful face
To feel the warmth it brings

Her wings spread apart
Like roses in the sun
Whispers shout from all around
She is a chosen one

Singing praises glorifying the king
Blessings flow upon her
For she is crowned with everlasting life
An Angel in the Midst of Angels

Crenisha Mone't Wright

Brenda A. Peacock

Copyright © 2003 **Crenisha Mone't Wright**

My mother didn't die; she laid her earthly suit to rest, waiting that glorious day when it will be raised in immortality at the coming of Christ Jesus. It's not a lost but a separation when a love one (Christian) departs this life. I didn't loose her; she's still with me in spirit, however I am saddened when I think of how I gave in to the devil by not fighting the good fight faith. Because I grew weary, faint, and drew back in the end, I didn't receive the promise, "Many are the afflictions of the righteous but <u>the Lord delivered him</u> from them all (Ps. 34:19)." How shall we escape if we neglect so great salvation?

I neglected to keep the promise in my heart: meditating therein day and night but her will and faith played a big part in the outcome. Jesus desired to heal all those that were afflicted but couldn't because of there disbelief: other hindrances include an unforgiving heart, strife, sin, and ignorance of the provisions, all of which is between that person and God. Through revelation knowledge of our Lord and Savior Jesus Christ we are given a way to escape the sins and attacks of the world. I've purposed in my heart that never again will God speak to me and I not adhere and obey.

With My Whole Heart

I'm not just a woman, and not just any woman, but a woman God can use, my heart is sold out to Him. Who can find such a virtuous one? Her price is far above rubies. Strength and honor are her clothes and her tongue is the law of kindness.

Entreat me not to leave thee, or to return from following after you; for where you send me I will go; and where you lodge I will lodge (Ruth 1:16). What character, submission, and love. Ruth's dedication to Naomi and to the God of Israel is exemplified in the above scripture. The basis of her devotion was love, which is the foundation of our faith. God is love and we must exhibit that love in its' fullness. When we accept Christ as Lord and Savior, we make a commitment to love and follow Him, and to go to all nations of the world, telling of the awesome love and power of God that changes lives: there is no one else who can do it.

The time has come and now is that we began walking in the calling for which we are called; repent, turn yourselves from your idols, and turn away your faces from all your abominations (Ez.14: 6b). O harlot, hear the word of the Lord: I will gather all thy lovers with whom thou has taken pleasure and loved. How weak is your heart seeing thou doest all these things, the work of an imperious whorish woman; as a wife that takes strangers instead of her husband. I will judge thee as women that break wedlock (Ez.16: 30,35-38).

We are a hardheaded, stiff hearted and rebellious nation that has rebelled against God: our children and fathers to this very day. But its' time we acknowledge what thus said the Lord and begin living the God kind of life. He is pleading with us face to face; purging the rebels and them that transgress against Him. Go serve your idols if you will not hearken unto me: pollute not my name any more: serve me and I will accept them. God has no pleasure in the death of the wicked; but that they turn from their ways and live. God warns us, say unto the wicked thou shall surely die; we will be held accountable if we fail to do so.

Woe to Us

To whom much is given much is required and we have a responsibility to share with others. It's not enough that we receive revelation; we have a responsibility to share what we know, and not leave anyone behind. God is searching for men and women to make up the hedge, and stand in the gap before Him that He should not destroy; can He find such a person in you? "Shepherds feed the flock. You eat and are clothed but feed not the flock." The true gospel of our salvation isn't being taught, leaving the sheep to wander in darkness, a prey for evil. The diseased are not strengthened, the sick are not healed, hearts are not minded, and we've not taken possession of the land and spoil therein.

Jesus is coming soon but not due to the condition of the world; the work of the devil won't factor in to the decision. God doesn't move or react to the wickedness of this world. He's watching and anxiously awaiting the purification of His bride (church); with such things as belong to her: and He preferred her (church) and she obtained grace and favor in His sight (Ester 2:9,17). A bride tried as silver purified by the earth; affliction laid upon her loins, men having ridden over her head; gone through fire but brought out into a wealthy place (Ps. 67:10-12). She will be a strong city; salvation will God appoint for walls and bulwarks (Is. 26:1). God who is sovereign and reigns forever has declared victory for us, and over all the works of His hands; Alpha and Omega, the

beginning and the end; declares what is, what was, and which is to come.

Brenda A. Peacock

Always In Prayer

Heavenly Father, you have declared in your word, you give us the heathen for our inheritance and the world for our possession. We believe therefore we speak and receive. We ask you Father, in the name of Jesus, to make known your will to those who diligently seek after you. Let your glory manifest in our lives and your marvelous works be known throughout the land.

Thank you father, in the name of Jesus, for the salvation of our families, love permeating in their lives and walking in obedience to your word: blind eyes being opened and deaf ears hearing when your Spirit speaks. Thank you for those you are bringing into the fold, family, friends, and those who consider themselves our enemies: none dying but all receiving the life you so graciously gave us in abundance. Thank you for our world leaders, give them a heart to seek your face and your peace for our country and abroad.

Thank you for wealth and riches that are in our houses/mansions that we did not build and riches when we did not labor; the transfer of wealth

from the hands of the wicked to the just, thereby enabling us to become distribution centers for the kingdom. Father, enlarge our territory and let your hand be with us always, supernaturally canceling debts (house, car notes, credit cards, loans and etc.), that we owe no man nothing but to love him and that our storehouse will overflow as a result of your blessing, which makes us rich and add no sorrow.

In Pursuit of Him

My heart is indicting a good matter. A matter between my lover and me: a spiritual love affair that transcends time, it cannot and will not end. I love Him with my whole heart, and with my whole heart I will love Him. Why, because I'm persuaded by His undying love for me.

God is in pursuit of my heart and I'm in hot pursuit of Him. Every moment I'm awake I desire to be in His presence. He consumes my every thought and fulfills my every need, and when I feel lonely I know I'm not alone. You see, I Know Him and He knows me. I know who I am in Him, and my name He knows because He made me; I'm His, and nothing without Him.

Psalms 119:
Father, I have thought much about your words, and stored them in my heart. Bless me with life. Open my eyes to see wonderful things in your word. Reassure me that your promises are for me, for I trust and revere you. In fairness renew my life, for this was your promise Lord, to save me! I am overflowing with your blessings, just as you said. I faint for your salvation; but I expect your help. My eyes are straining to see your promises come to me. In your kindness, spare my life; then I can continue to obey you. Forever, O Lord your word stands firm in heaven. Your faithfulness extends to every

generation; it endures by your decree, for everything serves your plans. You are my refuge and my shield, and your promises are my only source of hope. You promised to let me live! Never let it be said that God failed me. I have thoroughly tested your promises and that's why I love them so. Through the night I think about your promises and early in the morning, before the sun is up, I pray and point out how much I trust in you. I long for your salvation. I praise you for letting me learn your laws. Stand ready to help me because I have chosen to follow your will; let your laws assist me.

What are you waiting on? There's no better time than the present to be about the Fathers' business.

God made time for man and not for himself because he doesn't need it. It was given us to measure the span from the fall of man in the Garden of Eden, to the coming of the Messiah, and inevitably the reconciliation of Gods creation to himself. We're to do kingdom work, on our jobs, at school, work or play, waiting His return.

> **Time will change,**
>
> **When time will be no more and then,**
>
> **It will not be time, but eternity.**

This is the moment so take every opportunity to witness for Christ.

In hope of a new beginning for you

When We Pray

Hear the right O Lord, attend unto my cry; give ear unto my prayer that goes not out of feigned lips. Teach me to pray as you instructed the disciples:

Matthew 6:9-13

<u>Our Father which art in heaven</u>, you are our source and bloodline, the originator and creator of the universe. We are created in your image and likeness; beautifully and wonderfully made for His good pleasure. Great is the work of your hand, sought out by many. Supreme Being and head of the Trinity: Father, Son, and Holy Ghost, <u>Hollowed be thy name</u> Jehovah God;

> Jireh (provider), Shammah (always present), Sabboath (commander-in chief), Elohim (faithful in covenant), Shalom (peace), Tsidkenu (righteousness), M'Kaddesh (sanctifier), Emmanuel (with us), Rophe (healer), Rohi (shepherd), El Shaddi (more than enough), Wonderful, Counselor, Bread of Life, Rose of Sharon, Lilly of the Valley, Bright and morning Sun, I AM that I AM (all that we will ever need).

Thy kingdom, which is seedtime and harvest time, has come. We plant your word in our hearts and meditate day and night, the Holy Spirit in us providing wisdom and knowledge from above. Our hearts are filled with the abundance of your love therefore we speak life and not death over every situation, knowing that we have whatsoever we say; speaking it into existence with the words of our mouth. Father we only say those things we hear you say when we study your word, which is the blue print for our break through in the spirit realm, and heavens manifestation on earth. **Thy will be done**: fear the Lord thy God, walk in all His ways, to love and serve Him with all thy heart and soul, **on earth same as it is in heaven**. You know what we have need before we ask so we **thank you this day for our daily bread**; taking no thought what we shall eat, drink and wear, knowing that you give to us richly everything to enjoy. We don't worry about tomorrow because tomorrow will take care of the things for itself.

Forgive us our debts, rejecting you, disobedience, stiff necks, hard hearted, for the imagination of man's heart is evil from his youth Gen. 8:21. If I have wronged any man bring it to my remembrance, and **I forgive everyone** who has ought against me. Lead us not into temptation for our spirit is willing but our flesh is weak. You cannot be tempted neither do you tempt any man however the same serpent that beguiled evil is lurking today seeking whom he may devour: but you are faithful and will not suffer us to be tempted above that we are able; but will deliver us from evil (a way to escape). Defend my cause, O Lord, with them that strive with me; fight against them that fight against me. My heart will not faint, fear, or tremble because of the evil. A thousand shall fall at my side and ten thousand at my right hand but it won't come near me because I abide in you. **For yours is the kingdom, the power** (authority over all), **and the glory** (signs and wonders) in heaven and earth **forever.**

Amen.

About the Author:

Brenda is a born again spirit filled Christian. A native of Forrest City, Arkansas she currently resides in Texarkana, Texas. She earned a bachelors degree in elementary education with a specialist in special education from Henderson State University. Her job carrier includes 4 years of teaching and the remaining 22 working for the federal government. Brenda's education, work experiences and other training does not compare to the knowledge she received in preparation for this book, beyond comprehension. She is not a writer by any means, however by inspiration from the Holy Spirit, and a desire to let the world know how much she cherishes her personal relationship with the Father, she has put some of her experiences on paper.